WALKS ALONG THE SHORE

KAY CORRELL

ZURA LU PUBLISHING LLC

ABOUT THIS BOOK

Walks Along the Shore

There's a wedding at Blue Heron Cottages and everything possible is going wrong. Jill is the maid of honor—at fifty years old—and she's determined to give her best friend, Christie, the wedding she deserves. The problems with the wedding planner, the dress, the catering, a huge storm... these are all problems Jill can fix.

Maybe.

But the one thing she can't fix is the fact that her ex-boyfriend, Scott, is the best man.

Best man? Ha. He's the worst man ever. He broke her heart years ago.

But fate has a way of interfering and the past is not always as it seems. Secrets are revealed and Jill has to decide what she truly wants from life. It's never too late for a new beginning, or is it?

My newsletter subscribers got a bonus epilogue to this story. If you'd like to get the epilogue and other bonus content you can sign up for my newsletter here:

kaycorrell.com/bonus2

This is book two in the Blue Heron Cottages series. It will be at least six books… if not more. I have so many ideas for stories in this series!

Memories of the Beach - Book One

Walks along the Shore - Book Two

Bookshop near the Coast - Book Three

This book is dedicated to those people who find love later in life. Or have a second chance with a first love.

KAY'S BOOKS

Find more information on all my books at
kaycorrell.com

COMFORT CROSSING ~ THE SERIES
The Shop on Main - Book One
The Memory Box - Book Two
The Christmas Cottage - A Holiday Novella
(Book 2.5)
The Letter - Book Three
The Christmas Scarf - A Holiday Novella
(Book 3.5)
The Magnolia Cafe - Book Four
The Unexpected Wedding - Book Five

The Wedding in the Grove - (a crossover short

story between series - with Josephine and Paul from The Letter.)

LIGHTHOUSE POINT ~ THE SERIES
Wish Upon a Shell - Book One
Wedding on the Beach - Book Two
Love at the Lighthouse - Book Three
Cottage near the Point - Book Four
Return to the Island - Book Five
Bungalow by the Bay - Book Six
Christmas Comes to Lighthouse Point - Book Seven

CHARMING INN ~ Return to Lighthouse Point
One Simple Wish - Book One
Two of a Kind - Book Two
Three Little Things - Book Three
Four Short Weeks - Book Four
Five Years or So - Book Five
Six Hours Away - Book Six
Charming Christmas - Book Seven

SWEET RIVER ~ THE SERIES
A Dream to Believe in - Book One
A Memory to Cherish - Book Two

A Song to Remember - Book Three
A Time to Forgive - Book Four
A Summer of Secrets - Book Five
A Moment in the Moonlight - Book Six

MOONBEAM BAY ~ THE SERIES
The Parker Women - Book One
The Parker Cafe - Book Two
A Heather Parker Original - Book Three
The Parker Family Secret - Book Four
Grace Parker's Peach Pie - Book Five
The Perks of Being a Parker - Book Six

BLUE HERON COTTAGES ~ THE SERIES
Memories of the Beach - June 23, 2022
Walks along the Shore - September 13, 2022
Bookshop near the Coast - January 2023
Plus more to come!

WIND CHIME BEACH ~ A stand-alone novel

INDIGO BAY ~ A multi-author sweet romance series

Sweet Days by the Bay - Kay's Complete Collection of stories in the Indigo Bay series

Sign up for my newsletter at my website *kaycorrell.com* to make sure you don't miss any new releases or sales.

CHAPTER 1

Violet Bentley stood beside the reception desk at Blue Heron Cottages. "You sure you've got this?"

Aspen nodded. "I've got this. We have three cottages of guests checking in. You want the bride-to-be and maid of honor in the yellow cottage, the groom and best man in the mint green cottage next door. The bride's family in the pink cottage. If any other guests show up early, I have those cottages written out here on your list." Aspen grinned. "All color-coded by cottage."

Violet laughed. She was a *tiny bit* of an over-organizer. "Well, it's easy for the guests to remember which cottage they're in since I named each cottage by their color."

1

"Really, you should go into town and run your errands. I've got this." Aspen's eyes flashed with confidence.

Violet didn't know what she'd done before hiring Aspen to help her here at the cottages. It was so nice to be able to run errands knowing the resort was in capable hands. Aspen had picked up on everything so quickly.

She wavered, still uncertain if she should really leave. "I should go check the cottages to make sure they're ready before I leave."

"I already did that. And yes, before you ask, I put the bouquets of flowers in each one."

"I just want this wedding to go off without a hitch. I'm still not great with doing the whole run the resort and making sure the setup for the wedding is ready all at one time."

"That's why you should give me more to do." Aspen's brow furrowed. "No, seriously. I can do more. I *want* to do more."

"I'm not much of a delegator." It was one of her less charming traits. She always thought she had to do everything. Make sure everything was just right. But sometimes it overwhelmed her to be the only one in charge.

Her brother, Rob, walked into the reception area from the attached owner's suite they shared. "Hey, I thought you were headed into town an hour ago."

"I was. I mean, I am." She glanced at her watch. Had it really been an hour?

"She's busy double-checking that everything is ready for the wedding this week." Aspen defended her.

"You mean she's looking over your shoulder and double-checking any little task she's given you to do?" Rob rolled his eyes. "She's got double-checking anything you help her with down to an art form."

"I do not," she said indignantly. Though, to be honest, she did.

"Go to town. How about even grabbing a cup of coffee with Melody? Take a little break, sis."

"I don't have time for that."

"Yes, you do. I've got everything here covered," Aspen insisted. "I really do."

She let out a long sigh. "Okay, okay. You two quit nagging me. I'm outta here." And she knew they weren't nagging. Not exactly. But she doubted she'd take time to have coffee with Melody. She wanted to get back here and make sure all the guests were settled in and check and see if they needed anything.

"What's the use of hiring Aspen if you don't let her actually do anything? And she seems to have picked up on everything quickly. Let her work."

Okay, that was nagging.

"I *do* let her work."

Rob rolled his eyes yet again. It annoyed her when he did that. Which was probably why he did it so often.

"If I see you back before two hours have passed, I'm throwing you out," he threatened.

"You can't do that. I own the place." She glared at him.

"Just watch me." He shook his head as he disappeared back into the owner's suite.

"He's so bossy," she muttered under her breath as she gave Aspen a weak smile and headed out to her car.

Jill Sawyer tugged her suitcase from the trunk of her car and headed to the yellow cottage that waited cheerfully for her as if this wasn't going to be a long, drawn-out week. Aspen, the woman at the front desk, had told her she was the first to arrive from the wedding party. Fine by her. She wasn't sure she was ready for all of this, anyway. She'd just slip inside and hang out there as much as possible this week. Somehow she'd make it through this wedding and escape back home. Besides, she had a big business meeting next week. An important one. Maybe she could leave early on Sunday and head out. Yes, that was a great plan.

Oh, she was glad Christie and Tony were getting married. Well, kind of glad. She was happy for her best friend, but couldn't she have picked a different man to marry? One whose best buddy wasn't Scott Kenner?

Christie had been very straightforward when she'd asked her to be the maid of honor in the wedding. She said Scott would be the best man and asked if that would be a problem.

Jill, *of course*, had insisted it was no problem at all. Not even a little bit. Didn't bother her. Really, it was fine. Just fine.

All of that Scott drama was in the ancient past.

Christie had looked doubtful but hugged her with gratitude.

She figured she'd just avoid Scott as much as possible. Christie had always talked about having a big wedding at some fancy place.

Surely there would be lots of room to avoid Scott.

But then—after she'd already said yes—she found out Christie was having a *small* wedding. Forty people for a destination wedding at a small resort in Moonbeam, Florida. And the wedding party would be staying at the cottages at the resort. All of the wedding party. Which included Scott.

Forty people. Hard to avoid a person when there would only be forty people.

She swept her gaze around the courtyard surrounded by cottages. The cottages were, let's just say, not very far apart. And Aspen had cheerfully told her the groom and best man were staying at the mint green cottage right next door. She looked over and glared at the cottage that wasn't even a stone's throw away from hers.

She paused, wondering if she could go back and ask Aspen to move them to a different cottage. She raised her hand to shield her eyes from the glaring sun and looked across the distance. Like maybe that cottage all the way across on the other side of the courtyard.

"Hey, Jillybean."

She froze at the sound of his voice and his nickname for her. She gritted her teeth and dropped her hand as she turned around to face him. She couldn't stop her sharp intake of breath. She swore silently even though she wasn't the swearing kind.

He looked… annoyingly handsome. More good-looking as he aged. Just the tiniest bit of gray hair at his temple. Not carefully covered like her grays. His arms were tanned, and muscles bulged beneath his t-shirt.

"You just going to stand there staring at me?" He flashed one of the lazy grins he was famous for.

That grin. She'd almost forgotten that grin. Almost. "I… uh… hi." She sounded like an idiot.

"Looks like Tony and I have the cottage right next door."

Probably too late to see if they could build an eight-foot fence between the two cottages.

"Christie and Tony are about fifteen minutes behind me. They'll be here soon."

She cleared her throat. "Good. I can't wait to see Christie. It's been months." She'd avoided going back to her hometown, Sweet River Falls, a small town in the mountains just outside of Denver, as much as possible. Too many memories. Besides, she had no family left there, so what was the point?

"Yeah, Christie said you've been ghosting her."

"I have not." She put her hands on her hips, glaring at him. Besides, he had no right to judge her. None.

"She said you missed her bridal shower." He cocked his head.

"I got tied up at work. I video chatted with them, though."

"But you're the maid of honor." His voice was more matter-of-fact than accusing, but it still riled her.

"Like I said, I was tied up at work." But had she really been? What kind of maid of honor missed the bridal shower? No, she'd been busy. It had been impossible to get away. It had nothing to do with the fact that she'd heard Scott and Tony were meeting up with Christie and the other shower guests at Mac's Place after the shower. And that it was mostly a group of friends they'd grown up with. The exact group that knew what happened between her and Scott and gave her pitying looks the few times she'd come back to Sweet River. So, she'd solved that problem by rarely going back. It had been, what? Ten years now, maybe more. She did occasionally meet Christie for a weekend somewhere, and Christie came and visited her every other year or so. And they talked on the phone at least once or twice a month.

Why was she justifying all this in her mind? She had been busy with work. She was *always* busy with work.

Scott looked at her for a long minute, and she resisted the urge to squirm. "It's good to see you." He nodded as he picked up his suitcase and crossed the way-too-few feet to the mint-colored cottage. He turned and gave her a small wave as he went inside.

She took a long, steadying breath. At least that was over. The first time she'd laid eyes on Scott Kenner in more than thirty years.

And it annoyed her to no end that he looked so… good.

CHAPTER 2

Violet entered Parker's Cafe and waved to Melody, who was waiting on a customer. It was really Sea Glass Cafe, but the locals called it Parker's Cafe and she was beginning to feel more and more like a local. She slid onto a stool at the ice cream counter. Maybe she'd just have a piece of peach pie with a nice scoop of ice cream on top. She deserved that, didn't she?

Melody hurried over and squeezed behind the counter. "Violet, hi. Don't see you come in here very often."

"Now that Aspen is working for me, I thought I'd take time for a slice of pie while I was in town. I just got some supplies at the general store and decided I'd pop in here." And ice cream wasn't coffee, so she wasn't taking her brother's advice. So there.

"Ice cream on that?"

"Yes, of course. Love your ice cream."

"I think I'll join you. We're slow now." Melody came back with two slices of warm peach pie with huge scoops of ice cream slowly melting and caressing the golden crust.

She took a bite and let the tantalizing taste of peach, cinnamon, and vanilla linger. "I swear, this is like the best pie ever."

"I agree with you on that." Melody took a bite of hers. "Evelyn keeps trying to teach me how to make it, and I'm getting close, but still not as good as when she does it."

"Rob said he's put on ten pounds since they started dating. I swear he brings home slices of pies, or homemade bread, or some other delicious concoction every day."

"Those two seem to be getting very close. He's in here almost every day."

"He's made noise that he's going to move out of the owner's suite and into his own place. As much as he might be an annoying older brother, I'm not sure I'm ready for him to move. I kind of like having him around." She laughed. "But don't ever tell him that. He says I only like having him around to help out with things that break at the cottages. He is awfully handy."

"Living alone isn't all it's cracked up to be," Melody said. "Sure, you get to choose the TV station and make what you want for dinner. But… well… it gets lonely sometimes."

"I'm sorry, Mel. I'm sure it's been hard for you."

"It's been over two years. You'd think I'd be used to it by now." Melody let out a long sigh.

"I don't think there's a timetable for getting over the death of your husband. I think it just takes time."

She nodded. "It does get easier. Some. But some days… like today… I don't know. He's just been on my mind a lot today."

"Any particular reason?"

"Ah… yes. It's the anniversary of the date he asked me to marry him. I was so happy that day. I thought I had everything I ever wanted. I just had no idea how quickly it would all disappear."

She reached over and squeezed Melody's hand. "Sorry. I wish I had words that would make it better."

Melody gave her a little smile. "It helps to talk about him sometimes. Most people avoid saying anything about him anymore."

"You can always talk to me about him. I never met him, but I'm a good listener."

"Thanks, Violet."

She knew Melody still mourned the loss of her husband, but at least she'd had that great love in her life. Violet had never found that with anyone. And now, in her mid-forties, she wasn't sure she'd ever find it. Oh, she'd dated. Even seriously a few times. But no one had ever been *the one*. Not that her life wasn't full and good now. But sometimes she wished she could share it with someone. Someone other than Rob, that is.

Evelyn came out from the kitchen. "Violet, hi. Didn't know you were here. Would you mind taking some pot roast for Rob's dinner? I'll send some for you to have, too."

Violet looked at Melody and raised her eyebrows. "See, I told you. She feeds him all the time."

Evelyn laughed. "I love feeding him. I love feeding everyone. I'm happiest in the kitchen, baking or cooking. It brings me a lot of joy."

"I'll pop in the kitchen when I'm finished with my pie and get it for him."

"Great, thank you." Evelyn disappeared back into the kitchen.

"She's right about the joy thing, you know," Melody said. "I like working here at Parker's, I do. But I feel like… like I want something more. Something of my own. Something that brings as much joy to me as cooking does to Evelyn."

"Then you should try and find out what that is."

"I just have no idea." She shrugged. "But for now, I'm happy working here."

"A person should always do what brings them joy. My decision to buy the resort and remodel it was kind of sudden. And Rob thought I was a bit crazy to do it. But I love running the resort. Meeting new people. Owning my own business, even with its headaches and problems. It brings me joy."

"I hope to find that sometime."

"You will," she assured her friend, then turned as someone approached. "Hey, Ethan. Want to join us for pie?"

Ethan looked at Melody as if waiting for her to invite him, too. She jumped up. "Yes, join us. I'll go get a piece for you."

Ethan sat on the stool next to Melody's, a shy smile on his face. "Thanks for the invite."

"You bet." She smothered a grin. The man had better ask Melody out one of these days before someone else came in and swooped her up. Though today, with her melancholy memories, was probably not the best choice.

Melody came back and sat beside Ethan. "Glad you stopped by. Evelyn's pie is especially delicious today. You'll love it."

"I'm sure I will." Ethan smiled at Melody, and a slight blush crept across his cheeks.

Violet jumped up. "I have lots of errands to run and need to get back to the cottages. I'll see you two soon." She headed to the kitchen to get Rob's food, leaving the two of them to their own devices. Hopefully that would involve talking and figuring out they liked each other.

Violet got back to Blue Heron Cottages and went into the owner's cottage. "Hey Rob, Evelyn sent you dinner again. Pot roast."

"Great. You going to join me? She always sends over a healthy portion."

"Sure. In a bit. I need to take over the check-ins from Aspen. She has a dinner shift at Jimmy's." She closed the fridge door.

"Did you have coffee with Melody?" He raised an eyebrow.

"No, I did not." And she had no intention of telling him she *did* have pie and ice cream.

She walked into the reception area and Aspen was just greeting a guest. "Here, let me do that. You go and get ready for your shift at Jimmy's."

"Thanks, Vi."

Violet greeted the couple. "So, I guess you're the happy couple?"

The woman smiled. "Yes, Christie and Tony."

"I'm so happy you're having your wedding here. Your maid of honor and best man have checked in already. Here are keys to your cottages. Christie, you are in the yellow cottage. Tony, you're next door in the mint green cottage."

"Thank you." Christie reached for the keys.

"We have our part for your wedding all arranged. We just need to set up the arbor and the chairs. And back near the side, we'll have some bar height tables. And you're just having appetizers passed around, correct? Oh, and we'll have a table for the cake."

"Yes, that will be everything I'll need. My coordinator took care of everything else." The bride frowned at her phone. "She's supposed to come in today, too. But she's not answering my calls."

"Maybe she's just on the road and not where she gets good cell reception. It's kind of spotty in places on the way here."

"You're probably right. I'll try her other number at her office. Maybe her assistant will know how to get ahold of her."

"Make sure to let me know if you need anything."

"We will. Thanks." Tony slipped his arm around Christie's waist as they walked outside.

Violet bit her lip, going over all the details in her head, hoping she hadn't forgotten anything. She sure hoped everything went smoothly with the wedding. And with any luck, they'd add a review to her website. A little more social proof that the resort was a great place for a wedding.

CHAPTER 3

Jill jumped up as Christie walked into the cottage. Christie rushed over to give her a hug.

"You made it." She returned the hug, glad to see her friend. Christie's eyes sparkled with excitement.

"We did." Christie stepped back and rolled a huge suitcase into the cottage, then stepped outside again and grabbed another one, laughing. "I might have over-packed just a tiny bit."

"Maybe, but you can never be too prepared for a wedding."

"Speaking of prepared. I can't get a hold of my wedding coordinator. She's supposed to have all the arrangements made. I was so crazy at work that I figured hiring someone who had put together weddings before would be the smart way to go."

"Good plan."

"But I sure wish she'd call me back." Christie frowned at her phone as she set it on the table. "I still have some questions for her. She actually made the whole wedding a bit fancier than I'd planned or pictured in my head."

"This from the girl who talked nonstop about her big, fancy wedding when we were kids? The one in the big fancy hotel? Six bridesmaids. And miles of lace on your wedding dress?"

"Oh, my gosh, and remember when Darlene McGinnis heard me talking about all of that in high school? Not that I was dating anyone seriously at the time. She made so much fun of me."

"Darlene made fun of everyone. If you look up the definition of mean girl in the dictionary, there's a picture of her."

"Yeah, she was quite a piece of work. Remember when she told everyone you cheated on that math final when you got a perfect score?"

Did she ever. She'd spent weeks with people asking her if she really had cheated. "I wonder whatever happened to her."

"I don't know. She was around for a few years after high school, but then she just suddenly up and moved away. Haven't seen her since."

"Enough talk about Darlene. Back to how you always wanted that big wedding."

Christie shrugged. "What can I say? I grew up. And Tony and I decided we wanted a small, intimate wedding. Just family and a few friends. Though you know my family. It's huge. So that takes up most of the guests."

"I can't wait to see your mom and dad. Seems like it's been forever."

"It has been. You rarely come to Sweet River anymore."

"I know. I've just been crazy busy with work. Traveling a lot for work, too."

"I know. I just miss you." Christie gave her another hug. "But now I have almost a full week with you. It will be great."

"It will." Especially if the guys stuck to their own cottage.

A knock came from the door. "Come in," Christie called out.

Tony stepped inside, followed by Scott. So much for her hopes that the guys would stay in their own place. Tony gave her a big hug. Tony and Christie were huggers. Jill wasn't.

"So, what's the plan now?" Tony asked.

"I still can't get ahold of the wedding planner, but I've left messages for her. I'm sure she'll call back soon."

"So, you think we could go get something to eat? I'm starving." Tony patted his stomach.

"You're always starving," Christie teased.

"Growing boy. What can I say?"

Jill wasn't sure that a fifty-year-old man was considered a boy...

"I was reading a brochure in the cottage. There's a wharf here in town with a restaurant out on the end of it. Jimmy's. Want to go there?"

"Sure, that sounds nice." Christie nodded.

"You guys go ahead. I'm not very hungry." Jill had absolutely no intention of having dinner at the same table as Scott. None.

"Oh, come on. You can at least get a little something. We need to talk wedding stuff, anyway." Christie grabbed her hand and tugged. "You'll come with us." It was more of a statement than a question.

She smothered a sigh and put on a broad—if false—smile. "Of course."

"Let's go then. As I've already established, the men are starving." Tony laughed. "I'll drive."

She snatched her purse off the table and followed them all outside. Christie got into the front seat by Tony. Naturally. That only left her the back seat with Scott. He held the door open for her, and she avoided looking at him as she got in. And avoided noticing how close he sat next to her in Tony's compact car. Why couldn't the man have gotten a big old SUV where at least there'd be some distance between her and Scott?

Tony pulled out of his parking spot, and Jill crowded as close as possible to the car door. So far, things weren't going exactly as planned. And she was a planner. And liked things to go the way she planned them. She glanced over at Scott and saw he was giving her that lazy grin of his. Again. Like he was amused at her or something. She quickly turned away and looked out the window, totally ignoring him. Totally.

23

Aspen entered Jimmy's on the Wharf and went to search for Walker. She wouldn't mind a quick minute or so with him before her shift started. She found him in the office with his head bent over some paperwork. "Hey, you." She stood in the doorway.

He looked up and a smile spread across his face—one she wasn't quite used to, that was just for her—as he hopped up and came over to her. He wrapped his arms around her waist and pulled her close. "I've missed you," he whispered against her head as he held her tightly. "Why do you stay away so long?"

Her heart fluttered at his words, and she pulled back slightly. "You realize I just saw you last night, right?"

"Like I said, it's been forever." He leaned in for a long, lingering kiss.

A kiss that made her knees go weak as she clung to his arms.

"Ahem..." A voice came from behind her and she struggled to pull out of his embrace, but he held her tight.

"Go away, sis," Walker said, barely lifting his lips from hers.

"I have no desire to see my brother kissing someone. Even if he did wise up and start dating a great woman like Aspen. Although I'm not sure what she sees in him…"

"Get to the point, then run off and leave me to my kissing."

"I would, but Dad needs you out in the restaurant. And it's gotten busy. I need Aspen to clock in."

Walker slowly released his hold on her, a long sigh escaping his lips. "Looks like duty calls. We'll continue this later." He flashed a smile.

She turned to Tara, her cheeks flushed. "I'll clock in right away."

Tara shook her head, but a smile played on her lips. "You two. Always kissing. What am I going to do with you?"

"I suggest you mind your own business." Walker shot the words at his sister as he left the office.

"Like that will ever happen," she shot back and turned to Aspen. "I know I tease you guys, but I am really delighted for you two. I haven't seen Walker this happy since…" She paused and frowned slightly. "Well, since forever. And it suits him. But don't tell him I said that."

Tara slipped an arm around her shoulder. "Now come on. Let's get you started. I know you've been working the host station, but are you ready to start waiting tables?"

"Yes, of course."

"Perfect. Why don't you shadow me for a bit and I'll show you the ropes? But since you said you've been a server before, I don't think it will take you long to catch on."

Aspen was anxious to start waiting tables. The servers here said the tips were usually quite good, and she could use the extra money. Even with working two jobs, she worried about her finances.

Finances. Ha. She could hardly call her meager savings finances. They were basically non-existent. And she was determined to finally grow a healthy nest egg. She couldn't just drift from job to job her whole life, never having anything saved up.

Not that she planned on leaving Moonbeam anytime soon. First of all, there was Walker. And she had this job and the one at the cottages. And Violet had given her a cottage to stay in rent-free if she just worked on fixing it up. She planned on starting the painting this week. Violet had picked out a light blue color for the inside and an azure blue for the outside, to coordinate with the other brightly painted cottages. She wanted to get the outside painted first. The part other people would see and that would let Violet know she was keeping up with her side of the bargain. Then she'd tackle the inside.

Violet had told her about a place in Wind Chime Beach where there was a decorating store she'd heard about from a friend. It had fairly priced antiques. The two of them were heading up there soon to find some furniture to replace the rickety furnishings the cottage had now.

She couldn't believe all that had changed in her life since coming to Moonbeam. Finding out she had a sister. Falling for Walker—she still couldn't believe that. And him falling for her. His family practically adopting her and accepting her as one of them. And two jobs she loved. All in all, it had been a great couple of weeks.

"You ready?" Tara interrupted her thoughts.

"Yes," she answered as she grabbed a pad and pen to take orders.

"And Aspen? I'm really glad you showed up here in Moonbeam."

"Me, too." Happiness bubbled through her as she followed Tara out into the restaurant.

CHAPTER 4

Jill smiled with delight when they walked through the restaurant and saw the gorgeous view of the bay stretching out before them. Maybe she could just face the water the whole evening and ignore that Scott was here with them?

They were seated at a four-top table near the railing. She couldn't figure out any way to avoid sitting next to Scott—there were two seats on each side of the table—because, of course, Christie would sit next to Tony. Scott pulled out a seat for her and she reluctantly slid onto it. He sat right next to her. Too close. Just like in the car.

Christie grabbed her phone when it dinged. "Oh, it's Mom and Dad. They got a late start this morning and decided to stop and spend another night on the road. They'll be here tomorrow. Good. I worried that it was a long drive for them."

"That's probably a good idea," Jill agreed.

"Look, there's Aspen from the cottages. She must work here, too." Christie waved.

Aspen and another woman came over to the table. "Glad you all decided to try Jimmy's. Best restaurant in town," Aspen said. "This is Tara. Her family owns the restaurant. Tara, these are guests at the cottages."

"Jill." She pointed to herself. "Christie, Tony, and…" She turned and glanced briefly at Scott, who shot her that ridiculous grin of his. Which she ignored. "And Scott."

"Nice to meet you," Tara said. "Can we get drinks for you while you look at the menus?"

They ordered drinks, and Jill pored over the menu, ignoring Scott sitting right beside her. Bumping elbows occasionally. Annoying her. Couldn't he at least stay on his half of the table?

They ordered their meals when Aspen delivered their drinks.

"So, let's talk wedding," Christie said. "I can't believe it's finally here."

"The best thing about the wedding

happening is we can quit constantly talking about the wedding plans," Tony teased, but his eyes conveyed he didn't mind.

"Hey, I just want everything to be perfect." Christie lightly punched his arm.

"Whoever would have thought when we were all kids growing up together that you two would decide to tie the knot?" Jill asked. Although at one point, she had thought maybe she and Scott would end up together. But that sure hadn't happened. And now she could barely stand to be in the same room as him. She slid a bit further away from him.

"Yes, it took us a while. Tony was slow to ask me out. I'd almost given up on him." Christie grinned at him.

"Hey, it's a new world these days. You could have asked me out," Tony tossed back.

"Cheers to two of us finally getting married in our fifties." Jill raised her glass. Even though she hadn't turned fifty yet. Her birthday was this weekend, not that anyone would remember. She no longer got birthday cards and usually celebrated her birthdays by ignoring them.

Tony sent Jill a hard frown. "What?"

Why was her frowning at her?

"Yes, to finally getting married and lifelong

happiness," Scott said loudly as he raised his glass, clinking against Tony's glass and sloshing beer on the table. The two men exchanged a look that she couldn't quite figure out. Intense on Scott's part. Apologetic on Tony's. But then, she never really could understand men, anyway. Especially Scott.

"It just proves it's never too late to find love," Christie said as she touched her wineglass to Jill's. "Just wait, Jill. You'll find your soulmate. I just know it."

She doubted that. She wasn't even looking. A soulmate would have to creep up on her and bop her over her head like Little Rabbit Foo Foo to get her attention. And to do that, she'd have to actually do something besides work all the time. She had no time for relationships. Besides, she was perfectly happy with the way things were.

Well, except for the fact she had to spend this week with Scott.

She said hardly a word while they ate their dinner, but no one noticed. She just wanted the meal over and to head back to the cottages. Hopefully, the guys would go to their own cottage and she and Christie could have some time for girl talk. Or, if Christie and Tony wanted alone time, she would just grab her laptop and check her email. She was worried she was missing out on things at work this week.

She couldn't remember the last time she'd taken a week off work. She'd heard there was a pool going at the office on whether she'd actually take this week off. But she had. Christie was her best friend. Though she admitted some reluctance when she'd cleared her desk when she left her office.

She turned back to listen to the conversation going on around her. The one she was barely paying any attention to. Something about the wedding cake.

"Don't you agree?" Christie asked her.

She had no clue what Christie was asking, but it was always a good idea to agree with the bride. "Of course," she answered, wondering what she was agreeing to.

Scott raised an eyebrow. "Really? I thought you hated lemon cake."

"I… uh…"

"We could just do the vanilla cake." Christie's forehead creased.

"Or chocolate. That's my favorite," Tony chimed in.

"The decision has to be made in the

morning so the bakery knows which one to make." Christie's frown deepened.

"I think you should go with whichever one you want." Still safer to agree with the bride. And if it was a lemon cake, it was that many fewer calories she'd have at the wedding. Not all bad. Because cake was her weakness.

They finished their meal, left Jimmy's, and walked down the long wharf. Shops lined each side and people wandered in and out of the stores. "Hey, look. A souvenir shop. I want to pop in there and get a mug from Moonbeam." Christie tugged on Tony's hand.

"You've got about a hundred mugs from all over, you know." Tony gave her an indulgent smile.

"But this is where we're getting married, so I *need* one from Moonbeam."

"Of course you do. Come on. I'll buy it for you." He took Christie's hand.

"Jill and I will meet you at the end of the wharf," Scott said without asking her.

Tony and Christie disappeared into the shop. She stood awkwardly next to Scott. Why was he deciding what she would do? Maybe she should just duck into the store, too.

"You didn't want to go in, did you? It's crammed full of people."

It was jammed with customers. And no, she didn't really want to go in. But she also didn't like being told what she was going to do. Especially by *him*.

"If we duck out the side, we can walk along the marina. Come on." He took a few steps toward the cut-through to the marina.

She still stood by the entrance to the shop, wavering. Did it really look that crowded inside? She peered through the window and saw the long line of people waiting to check out. Ugh.

"You coming?" Scott paused and looked back at her.

She reluctantly followed him, and they walked slowly beside gleaming white yachts and sailboats moored to the dock. At the end of a far dock, a huge double-decker boat called The Destiny was tied up. Almost every space at the marina was filled.

She concentrated on looking at the many boats as they walked, ignoring that Scott was just inches from her side. She silently read their names. Seas the Day. Lady Isabella. Not on Call. The Stella. How did people ever decide on names for their boats? Or names for their beach houses, for that matter. The streets were lined with named houses here in Moonbeam. Beach Happy, Endless Summer, Sea Haven. On and on. She hadn't even been able to come up with a name for a cat they'd adopted when she was a child. The kitty ended up being called Pink all its life after the color of her collar...

Scott finally paused and touched her arm so she'd stop. "Jill, you going to be okay this week? I mean, with me being here? Christie said she'd talked to you and you were fine. But you sure don't act like you're fine."

"I'm fine. Perfectly fine," she said automatically.

"You don't look it."

"I'm fine," she repeated, more to convince herself than him.

"I just don't want any of our... our stuff... our history... to get in the way of Tony and Christie's wedding."

"No, of course, it won't." But would it? No, she'd make sure it didn't.

"It was a long time ago." He looked at her intently.

"It was. Ancient history. Forgotten." And yet, it wasn't forgotten. When she had a weak moment and took the memories out, it cut her to her very soul. Not that she'd ever admit that to anyone. Especially Scott.

Wanting to end the conversation, she turned and continued to walk down the dock and left Scott to jog to catch up with her.

CHAPTER 5

The next morning, Jill and Christie sat out on the porch having much-needed mugs of steaming coffee. Violet had provided a bag of freshly ground coffee beans from a local shop and the flavor and aroma were excellent. Jill needed her coffee first thing. Usually she took a to-go cup as she raced into work.

The air wrapped around them like a damp blanket with no breeze to stir even a single palm branch. Who knew it would be this warm in September? Didn't Florida know it was fall? It showed all the promise of a hot, sticky day.

"Tony's not much of an early riser. He probably won't be up for another hour or so." Christie sat in her chair, sipping her coffee, looking all relaxed, which Jill thought was unusual since her friend was getting married in a few days. Weren't brides supposed to be panicked about now?

And she was fine with the guys sleeping in. She remembered Scott as an early bird but hoped he didn't decide to come out on his porch and spy them. She just wanted to enjoy some peaceful moments. You know, ones without Scott in them.

"Did you have a good time last night? It looked like you and Scott got along okay."

Scott, Scott, Scott. He was everywhere. But at least she'd fooled her best friend. "Sure, I told you everything would be fine." Just fine. She just had to keep repeating that to herself.

"I still didn't get a message back from the wedding coordinator. Do you think it's too early to call?"

"No, go ahead. Try again."

Christie took out her phone and dialed, setting it on the table between them on speaker.

A man's voice answered on the third ring. "Hello?" The word came out harshly, angrily.

"I'm trying to get ahold of Elizabeth."

"You and the other dozen or so phone calls I've gotten. She's gone."

"What do you mean, she's gone?" Christie frowned.

"Disappeared. Gone. Poof."

Jill took in a quick breath. Was the man saying the woman was missing?

"But she's planned my wedding. She knows all the arrangements." Christie's eyes widened, and she picked up the phone, grasping it with trembling fingers.

"I wouldn't plan on those arrangements being made. The bank account is empty. She's gone. I found out she's flown to South America. Good luck with finding her."

"But…" Shock settled on Christie's features.

"And don't count on her having made any of the arrangements she said she did. Your deposits were probably in that cleared-out account and not sent to the vendors. At least from what I can tell by all the angry brides calling this phone."

"I don't understand…" Christie's brows knitted together.

"Hey, don't feel so bad. I'm her husband, and she took off with every penny of our savings. And took out a loan against our home, too. You're in better shape than I am."

"I... I don't know what to say." Christie looked over at her in panic.

"Me either. But hey, good luck with your wedding." Heavy sarcasm dripped from each word, then the phone went silent.

Christie stared at the phone as if it were its fault it delivered the bad news, then looked up at her. "Now, what are we going to do?"

"I... I'm not sure. We'll figure something out."

Just then, Tony and Scott came out of their cottage and walked over. Tony took one look at Christie and asked, "Hey, you okay?"

"She's not okay. The wedding coordinator disappeared. With all the deposits you paid for everything. Which were never deposited with the vendors, by the way."

"No. Are you sure?" Tony's eyes widened in shock.

"Yes, we're sure." Jill nodded as Christie's eyes filled with tears.

Tony slid his arm around Christie's shoulder. "Ah, babe."

"We're supposed to get married Sunday. And... I have no wedding. No flowers. No food. No music. Oh... and no photographer. And she took off with our money."

"You could always reschedule," Scott suggested as he climbed the stairs to the porch.

Jill sent him a nasty glare.

"I don't want to reschedule. I waited my whole life for this."

Jill leaned forward and took Christie's hand. "Okay, then. We'll have to just figure this out. Do it all ourselves. We can do this. I bet we can." She wasn't actually sure they could pull this off, but she wasn't saying that to Christie. She shot a quick glance at Scott, imploring him to jump in with encouragement, but he just lounged against the railing, looking doubtful.

"Jill is right. We'll just have to do it ourselves." Tony squeezed Christie's shoulders. "We can do this." But he didn't sound very sure of himself either. More like he was just trying to keep Christie from panicking. Now she was seeing the panicked bride she expected earlier.

"The coordinator was making the wedding a bit fancier than I'd hoped. Always asking for more deposit money. Guess now we know why." Christie still had a dazed, sad expression on her face.

"Now we'll be able to make it exactly how you want it. Simple, if that's what you want."

43

"I do. But how can we do all this in just a few days?"

Jill glanced over at Scott again, annoyed at his uninterested expression. "Scott and I can figure this out. We'll make a list. Split things up. We'll get it all done."

"Me?" He shot her an incredulous look. "I don't know anything about planning weddings."

"Don't worry. I'll tell you what to do."

"Oh, that will be great," he muttered, not quite under his breath.

CHAPTER 6

Jill headed to the reception area to talk to Violet. Better to get a local's ideas on trying to figure out this whole wedding at the last-minute thing. She stepped inside, and Violet looked up from where she was having coffee with an older woman.

"Jill, can I help you?"

"I sure hope so." Jill plopped down on a chair beside them.

"Jill, this is Rose. She's staying in the Peach Cottage. The one at the end nearest the beach. Rose, this is Jill. She's here for her friend Christie's wedding."

"Glad to meet you. And a wedding. How nice." Rose's face lit up with a friendly smile, the wrinkles deepening around her blue eyes.

45

The color of the woman's eyes reminded Jill of her grandmother's Delft Blue pottery vase, a prized possession that sat on her bookshelf between her copy of *Alice in Wonderland* from the early nineteen hundreds and a worn copy of *The Power of Positive Thinking*. She jerked her thoughts away from her bookshelf. "About the wedding. It seems like the wedding coordinator didn't exactly do her job."

"How not exactly?" Violet asked.

"Like not at all. We found out she fled the country with a bunch of brides' money. We don't even think she contacted anyone or put down any of the deposit money Christie gave her."

"Oh, no." Rose frowned. "When is the wedding?"

"Sunday. I promised her we could figure this out. Still pull it off." She opened a small notebook. "But I'll need some help. Names of people to contact. I need everything. She was planning on just having appetizers. And a wedding cake, of course. And I'll need to figure out flowers if we can at the last minute. And a photographer." She shook her head. "And who knows what else I'm forgetting?"

"I'd be glad to help if I can." Rose offered.

"That's so kind of you. I'm sure not going to turn down any help."

"We at least have the chairs and arbor all arranged. The resort provides that." Violet's forehead creased.

"I don't suppose the coordinator actually paid you the venue deposit for the wedding, did she?"

"Only a part of it. Said the bride was bringing the rest with her." Violet grimaced. "I'm not the best businesswoman yet. It's all new to me. I know I shouldn't have scheduled it without all the money, and I didn't know how to ask Christie when she showed up. I just figured she'd pay the rest. But you know? Don't worry about that. She has enough to worry about. Let's just get this figured out."

"I'll talk to Tony. I'm sure he'll pay you the rest of the fee."

"Let me call my brother's girlfriend, Evelyn. She owns part of Sea Glass Cafe. Best cook and baker in town. I'll see if she can help with the food and cake."

"That would be wonderful."

"And she's planned so many events here in

47

Moonbeam. I bet she has suggestions for all the rest of your list." Violet pulled out her phone and called. "She's not picking up. I'll leave a message."

"If you can find the flowers, I can make the arrangements and bouquets for you and the bride. I worked in a floral shop for years," Rose offered. "I'd love to help."

"Wow, that would be wonderful."

"There's a floral shop over on Belle Island, Flossie's Flower Shop. I've gotten flowers for the resort from there before. Good prices."

"Great. I'll try that if Rose is willing to make up the arrangements."

"I can't think of anything nicer than helping with a wedding."

"I hate taking up your vacation time with work."

"It's no problem. I'm here for a few weeks. Just... taking some time away. I have nothing but time on my hands. Be glad to help. Why don't you let me call the floral shop and see what availability they have? See what kind of flowers are in stock now that we could use."

"That would be great. I know little to nothing about flowers. I do know Christie said she wants simple." The panic Jill had been feeling began to settle. Well, a tiny bit. She furiously jotted down notes.

"I'll come see you after I talk to Evelyn. Then I'll be able to give you some names and places to contact."

"Thank you." Jill popped up out of her chair. "I should run. I'll tell Christie I made progress on some of this."

"I'm sure Evelyn will be able to help you. And I'll do what I can, too." Violet got up and walked her to the door. "Tell Christie I'm sorry about all this."

"I will." Jill stepped out into the sunshine and headed toward the cottage. As she crossed the courtyard, she saw Scott standing at the edge of the beach, staring out at the waves. *Great, just take some beach time. It's not like we don't have a million things to do.*

By afternoon Evelyn had called her and given her the name of a photographer with availability this weekend. She and Christie had looked at his website and loved his work, so that was booked. They were lucky he'd had a cancellation this weekend. Some bride had called off her wedding at the last minute. Too bad for that bride, but good for them.

Evelyn agreed to do food for the wedding

but didn't have time to make the cake. But she did know the name of a bakery on nearby Belle Island, just across the bay. The owner, Julie, said she'd have time to make the cake, and Jill scheduled time tomorrow to go over and pick it out.

At least *a few* things were falling into place.

She sat out on the porch, scribbling notes in her notebook while Christie sat beside her, her stunned expression from this morning starting to ease away as each new plan was made.

Christie and Tony were meeting with Evelyn in the morning to pick out the menu, so that was done. Jill put a dot by it on her list. She'd check it off tomorrow when it was completed.

Hmm... it looked like everyone in the wedding party was doing something except Scott... But then, what did she expect? He wasn't the jump-in-and-do-stuff kind of guy. He was laid back... in the worst way. Just taking things as they came. It had always driven her mad the way he didn't make plans, or lists, or even really have much ambition. He insisted he was just easygoing. Ha.

She'd been all about plans their senior year of high school. They'd planned to go to the

University of Colorado in Boulder together. But then she got accepted *and* a scholarship to Wharton in Pennsylvania. They had a highly ranked business school, and she couldn't just pass that up. Scott agreed. He didn't even seem very upset that she was going way across the country, which irritated her. After all, they'd dated steadily for three years. But she'd been so busy at college and hadn't had the money to come home until Christmas.

That first Christmas back in Colorado. It had been... terrible.

Her thoughts were interrupted by a horn beeping. She turned to see Christie's parents pulling in.

Christie jumped up and rushed to the car. "Oh, Mom. You won't believe what happened."

Her mother got out of the car and hugged her. "What?"

"I don't have a wedding. Nothing was planned. The coordinator is in South America."

"What?" Her father frowned as he walked around the car and hugged her, patting her on the back. "Slow down. Now explain what happened."

"Hi, Mr. and Mrs. Palmer." Jill stepped up

to explain. "There was a bit of a mess-up. It appears the wedding coordinator ran off with their money and made none of the arrangements she said she had."

"Oh, no." Mrs. Palmer's eyes widened. "What are you going to do?"

"Don't worry. I've made some headway on plans. Christie is still going to have her wedding."

"At least I have a dress." Christie peered into the back seat of her parents' car. "Where is it?"

"About that." Her mother stepped back and ran her hands along her sides, then glanced nervously at Mr. Palmer. "Ah… the bridal salon had a bit of a problem."

"What kind of problem?" Christie eyed her mom.

"They had a couple people out with the flu. The alterations didn't get done on time."

"But what am I going to do?" Christie wailed.

"They promised to get it finished and overnight it. Everything will be fine. Don't worry, dear," Mrs. Palmer said, trying to placate her daughter.

Jill's heart skipped. She couldn't believe there was yet *another* problem.

But no matter what, she was going to make this wedding happen, and it was going to be great. She hated to fail at anything. It would be a perfect wedding. It would.

She hoped…

CHAPTER 7

S cott stood at the edge of the beach, letting the waves rush over his feet, but they did nothing to change the situation. The last place Scott wanted to be was at a wedding. The very last place.

But it was too late to back out now. He'd hesitated when Tony asked him to be best man, but how could he say no to his best friend? He figured all he had to do was help Tony get dressed, stand up there with him, then give a toast at the reception. And since he and Tony made up the groom's half of the wedding party, the bachelor party was just going to be a handful of beers at one of the bars in town. He could do that.

So, he'd said yes.

What a mistake that had been. Because then he'd found out Christie asked Jill to be the maid of honor. Jill. So many thoughts about her.

It surprised him that Jill had never married. She rarely came back to town, so there wasn't much gossip about what she was up to now. He'd figured she'd married, settled down with some rich, professional guy, and had two kids and a nanny. Not that he really thought about her. Well, some, but not often.

And yet... she was still single.

Now Jill wanted to throw him in the middle of wedding plans. Like smack in the middle. He wasn't even comfortable being *in* the wedding, much less helping to organize the thing. Why did she always make his life so complicated?

He hated weddings. Hated them.

And yet, here he was.

At one point, he thought he and Jill might marry. But he hadn't gotten up the nerve to ask her before she went away to her fancy college while he stayed home and went to the community college, leaving their plans to go to the University of Colorado behind him. He didn't want to go there without her.

Then, everything had fallen apart. And he'd made the biggest mistake in his life.

Well, maybe it was the second biggest. He seemed to make a lot of really bad choices, even if he was *trying* to do the right thing.

No, weddings were not his thing.

Maybe he could come down with the flu. Have a family emergency back home. Hide until the actual day of the wedding.

Maybe he was just a coward when it came to weddings…

He picked up a shell and threw it out into the ocean, but he knew he couldn't just stand here all day. He should go help with this whole fiasco, even if it was the last thing he wanted to do.

"If only I could go back and change the decisions I made," he whispered softly across the waves.

He swore the waves laughed at him.

Jill begged off on going to dinner that night. One less time she'd probably be forced to sit by Scott. It was so much nicer when she could just avoid him. Christie promised to bring a sandwich back for her. That suited her just fine. She wasn't that hungry, anyway.

She worked on her to-do list some more, checking on wedding websites for the ultimate do-all-this-for-your-wedding list. Besides, what did she really know about planning weddings? Nothing. And she didn't want to miss something obvious.

And she still had to write a speech for the reception, too. So much to do. She shut the lid on her laptop, took off her glasses, and rubbed her eyes. Slipping the glasses back on, she eyed the to-do list taunting her.

After standing and stretching, she decided that what she really needed was a quick walk on the beach. That would help clear her mind. Then she'd come back and tackle the planning again.

She slipped outside and headed to the shoreline, slowly walking down the beach as the sun began to set. The sky burst into brilliant colors of orange and a bruised purple.

She paused, awed by the sight. When was the last time she'd stopped to watch a sunset? Okay, last night at Jimmy's she'd kind of watched it, but that had been more of a distraction from the fact she was sitting right next to Scott.

Most of the time she didn't even get out of work until way after the sun had set, and she hadn't quite made it to the level at her company where she'd get an office with lots of windows. Her office had one tiny high-up window. Not that she took time to look out of it.

She frowned and thought about the accounts she'd left in her coworkers' hands while she was gone. Though she'd reiterated a million times that they could call her with any questions. And she'd checked her email at least a dozen times today, handling things quickly in between wedding planning.

She started to reach for her phone to check once again, then shook her head. What was she doing? *Look at this sunset.*

She sank down on the sand, determined to enjoy every moment of the magical display out over the water. She was kind of proud of taking this time for herself, avoiding work, avoiding the wedding. Just taking time for herself. Now *that* was kind of magical in and of itself.

"Hey, looks like you begged off dinner

tonight, too." Scott appeared at her side and the magic disappeared in a poof of disappointment.

How did he do that? *Why* did he do that? Just when she was relaxing and enjoying herself. "I, uh… wasn't very hungry."

"Yeah, me neither." Uninvited, he plopped down on the sand beside her.

Great. Just great. She ignored him.

"Tony said he signed me up to go over to some island tomorrow to pick out cake. I told him I wasn't a wedding cake expert."

She glanced over at him. "So, are you going?"

"He said it would involve tasting. I can taste cake." He grinned. "But I'll leave it up to you to pick out the design and details and everything."

Little did he know, *she* was also going to be the one to pick out the flavor of the cake. Not him. Besides, she knew Christie loved lemon cake. Or maybe a white cake with raspberry. She'd see what Julie had to offer. But *she* was making the decision. Not Scott.

"It sounds like you sure got a lot figured out today. But then you always were good with your lists."

"Planning and lists are how things actually get done." The words came out harsher than needed, but she was still annoyed he'd interrupted her peaceful personal time. She turned away from him—hoping he'd take the hint—and stared out at the waves, silently counting them as they broke near the shore.

"I'm not much of a planner."

"That I remember." She still ignored him, not even one little glance at him. Well, maybe one.

The setting sun highlighted his hair. His face was tanned, but that wasn't surprising. He loved being outdoors. There were the tiniest threads of gray at his temples. And the laugh lines by his eyes had deepened over the years.

"You done staring at me?"

"What? I'm not staring at you."

"Yes, you are." He quirked an eyebrow. "So, do you think I've changed?"

"I doubt it." She swiveled her head and watched the waves roll to shore, starting her count again. One. Two. Three.

"I meant my looks."

"Nope, still the same."

"You've changed. You look…"

She swiveled her gaze back to him. "Look what?"

"I was going to say older, but then I thought better of it."

"Just what every woman wants to hear. She looks older."

"No, I knew it wouldn't come out right. I've never been good with words."

No kidding.

"You look better. Age agrees with you."

Well, that was a little bit okay. Kind of.

"You're still beautiful."

Her mouth dropped open.

He grinned. "And it appears I can still surprise you."

That he could.

"So, the wedding. We still have a lot to do." She abruptly changed the subject back to safe territory.

Scott's long sigh stabbed through the air.

"You got a problem with Christie and Tony getting married?" She raised her eyebrows.

"No, of course not."

"Then why the long sigh?"

"I'm not a fan of weddings."

"I remember," she said pointedly.

"I…" He bent his head for a moment, staring at his hands, then looked directly into her eyes so intensely she almost flinched. "I'm sorry about all that. How it ended."

"*It* didn't end. You called everything off. You broke my heart."

"I know. And I'm so sorry."

An apology seemed so shallow after all these years. It wouldn't erase the pain she'd felt. The disappointment. The embarrassment.

"So… am I the reason you never got married?" He wouldn't break the connection of their eyes.

No, she wouldn't let him have the satisfaction of knowing he'd messed her up so badly. Hadn't trusted another man for years and years.

And then, any time she started to get serious with a guy, she'd find a reason they weren't right for each other. It was safer that way. Protected her heart from being shattered again. She would never let that happen again. Ever. And so far she'd successfully avoided any serious commitments.

And it wasn't that she'd been comparing them all to Scott. Certainly not. Nor was she comparing to the feelings she'd had for Scott. The feelings he'd trampled into a million tiny pieces.

"Am I the reason?" he asked again.

"No, just never found the right person." Never found the right person *again*. Then again, he'd been the wrong person since he'd broken her heart. Better back then than a bunch of years into a marriage.

"Oh."

She looked at him. "You're not married either." Why was he acting like she was an anomaly? She was so tired of people wondering if she was ever going to get married. Did they all think being married was the only way to find happiness?

His eyes held a brief moment of anguish. But she'd known him well enough all those years ago to recognize the pain, even if he quickly covered it up. "No, I'm not married."

"Did you ever get close to marrying?" she pushed, watching his face.

"Ah, that's a hard question to answer."

"And that's a non-answer."

"It will have to do. Can we talk about something else?"

The tiny flicker of pain flitted through his eyes again and he turned his face from her, scooping up a handful of sand and letting it sift through his fingers.

Okay, so he wasn't going to open up to her. That was *fine* with her.

She didn't care about what happened to him since he'd broken her heart. It's not like they were even friends anymore. Just two people trying to pull off a wedding for their best friends. You know, if Scott actually decided to be much help.

CHAPTER 8

Jill couldn't sleep, so she slipped out of the cottage early the next morning to let Christie sleep in. Though it was hard to walk away from the coffee that was begging her to make a pot. But she was afraid it would wake up Christie, and after all, she was the bride and needed her sleep.

She could wait until later for coffee.

Probably.

She scooped up her notebook and walked out onto the porch. The sky above was a light pink color, and not a palm frond stirred in the still, quiet air. The sun was just beginning to poke its way through a dotted patch of clouds. The door was open to the office, so she headed over that way. Maybe Violet had coffee…

"Hey, Jill," Violet said as she entered the office. "Want some coffee? I always have a pot brewed in the morning for any guests that want some."

"You're a mind reader. I sure do." She nodded more vigorously than she meant to. Violet laughed and within moments pressed a hot, steamy cup into her hands.

"Ah, thank you."

"Looks like everyone wants coffee today." Rose entered the office. "I've been out watching the sunrise, but then I thought I heard coffee calling my name."

"A woman after my own heart." Jill smiled at Rose.

Violet retrieved another mug. "Come on. Let's sit and enjoy the daybreak. I love this time of day."

They moved out to the porch, and Jill sank onto one of the rockers. "This is like the perfect start to a day. Coffee. Warm weather. Sunshine."

"It seems to always be a perfect morning in Moonbeam." Rose lifted the mug to her lips and took a sip. "How are the wedding plans going?"

Ah, yes. The wedding plans. Maybe not the perfect start to the day. Because the day entailed a trip to Belle Island with Scott. "They are coming along. I'm still so grateful that you can do the flowers."

"And Christie liked my idea of the daisies and a few yellow roses?"

"She loved it. Simple and pretty."

"And we'll do vases of daisies with a bit of greenery in them on the tables. I've told the florist we'll pick up the flowers Saturday morning. That will give me time to make all the arrangements."

"And we'll have to put them in everyone's fridges overnight Saturday so they'll be fresh on Sunday," Violet said. "So Christie doesn't have to worry about the flowers anymore."

"I really appreciate all the help." She took another sip of the coffee, the list of to-dos nagging her, and she sighed. "This is going better than I thought when we found out there were no wedding plans made. I really want this to work out for Christie. She's waited a long time to get married. Once we both got close to fifty, we had pretty much given up on the whole marriage idea. But then, after all these years of being friends, Tony and Christie started dating. Realized their feelings for each other."

"It's never too late to fall in love," Rose said.

"It gives me hope, then." Violet laughed. "I've never even gotten close to marriage, and I'm only a few years behind you on approaching fifty. I don't think it's in the cards for me."

"You never know. Sometimes love finds you when you least expect it." Rose set her cup down.

"Well, I'm not looking for it. I don't believe it's all it's cracked up to be." Jill shook her head.

"I'm not particularly looking for someone, either. I'm so crazy busy with the resort right now. But I wouldn't actually turn it down if love decided to come waltzing my way." Violet smiled.

She doubted love was ever going to waltz up to her, but she'd made her peace with that years ago.

"Love can be a wonderful thing when you find the right person to share your life with." Rose turned her head to look across the courtyard, a faraway expression in her eyes.

It was that finding the right person thing that was so hard to do. Not that she was looking. She stood, wanting to get away from this talk about finding forever love. "I better run. I have so much to do today. Thanks for the coffee."

She drained the last sip, and Violet took the empty mug from her.

"You're welcome. There's coffee here every morning."

She headed back to the cottage and found Christie up, dressed, and a fresh pot of coffee all made. Perfect. She poured herself another cup. She needed all the fortification she could get to make it through today.

"So, you and Tony are going to finalize the food today, right?" She sat down at the table and took out her notebook.

"We are. We're meeting with Evelyn mid-morning after the breakfast rush at the cafe. Honestly, I'll be happy with whatever she can come up with. I'm just so glad I'll actually have food at the wedding."

"You sure you don't want to come and pick out the cake?"

"I'd love to, but since Evelyn and Julie are doing this on such short notice and this morning was best for both of them, we'll just have to do it this way. Besides, you know me almost better than I know myself. I trust you to pick out the cake. And Tony…" Christie rolled her eyes. "Is very interested in the food. I swear he thinks it's the most important part of the wedding. Evelyn said she had a few things for us to taste and then we'll go from there."

Christie's phone rang, and she looked up, her eyes worried. "It's the bridal boutique."

"Answer it. They're probably calling to say the dress is on its way. Give you a tracking number."

Christie set the phone on the table and hit speaker. "Hello?"

"Ah… yes. May I…" The woman cleared her throat. "May I speak to Christie Palmer, please?" The nervousness in the voice was hard to ignore.

"Speaking." Christie shot her a questioning look.

"I'm sorry to say, but there has been a mix-up with your dress."

"I know. A delay with the alterations. But my mother said you were finishing it and overnighting it to me."

"That's where the problem comes in. We did finish it. But there was a mix-up on the shipping labels. I'm afraid your dress was shipped to the wrong bride."

"Can't you call her and have it shipped here?"

"Well… it was shipped to Paris. I'm afraid

there's not time for it to get to Europe and then back to you."

"Paris! My dress is in Paris?"

"Yes, I'm afraid so. I'm so sorry. Something like this has never happened to us."

Jill thought it was happening to *Christie*, not the bridal salon, but didn't interrupt.

"If you were here in town, we'd let you try on every gown here and make sure you'd have one for your wedding."

"But I'm in Florida."

"I realize that. I'm so sorry. We'll of course refund your money."

Like that would make any difference to Christie at this stage.

"We are sorry. I hope you can find another dress."

Christie just sat there with a stunned expression, staring at the phone.

Jill scooped up the phone. "This is totally unacceptable."

"We know. But there isn't really anything we can do at this point."

"Right. Thanks for letting us know." Jill clicked off the phone and turned to Christie.

"I can't get married without a dress," Christie whispered, a defeated look on her face.

"You won't have to. We'll find you another. One you love just as much," Jill said encouragingly.

"I'll never find one I love as much as that dress."

Just how many things could go wrong with one wedding? Jill clung to her encouraging smile. Did it look genuine? "We'll find one you love. I promise." Why was she promising? Who could find a dress in just days?

"I don't want to get married in just any old dress. It has to feel... right. You know? And when I looked at dresses before, so many were just too formal or too frilly or too... not me. Just... too."

"I know." She squeezed her friend's hands. "Tell you what. After you and Tony get done with Evelyn and I get back from Belle Island, we'll go dress shopping. Maybe into Sarasota? There's St. Armand's Circle. I'll talk to Violet and see where she suggests we go."

"I don't know why everything fell apart. You don't think it's some kind of sign, do you? Like I'm not supposed to be getting married?" Christie's forehead wrinkled.

"Don't start talking crazy. Of course you're supposed to be getting married. You guys love each other. I don't know why it wasn't obvious years ago that you two are meant for each other. So, enough of that kind of talk. We'll find a dress. I promise." She was making so many promises this week that she had no idea if she could keep.

CHAPTER 9

"I'll drive." Scott more or less commanded as they stood outside, ready to leave for Belle Island.

"No, *I'll* drive," she countered.

He looked at her skeptically. "Have you gotten to be a better driver than you used to be?"

Okay, so she'd had two car accidents when she was a teen. Lots of teens had accidents. And there was that *tiny* fender bender last year. "I don't know what you're talking about," she lied.

"I'll drive, you can navigate. Then you'll be able to tell me what to do. You like that." He flashed a sassy grin that made his eyes sparkle. Not that she cared.

She sighed. "Fine."

They got in Scott's car and headed across the bridge over Moonbeam Bay, then over to Belle Island. The weather was nice, and they rode along with the windows down. The wind tried to tug locks of her hair out of her precisely pulled-back ponytail.

A few years ago, she'd gotten her hair cut shorter, thinking since she was headed toward fifty, long hair wasn't the proper hairstyle for her. Or some silly notion. The cut had skimmed her shoulders, and she'd hated it. She had to mess around with it each day, trying to make it look nice and professional.

She'd never been happier than when it grew out and she could pull it back again. A nice, neat knot of hair was exactly the look she preferred. Professional. Put together. She should have taken the time to twist it into a knot today. Maybe that would have held its own against the wind. She considered asking Scott to put the windows up, but he'd for sure laugh at her if she complained it was messing up her hair.

They rode most of the way in silence except for her firing off directions. He sent her an annoying grin each time she gave him a direction.

Scott parked in front of The Sweet Shoppe. "We're here."

Mr. Obvious. It was a cute storefront. Inviting. And they could make the cake. What's not to like? She launched herself out of the car, ignoring Scott coming around to open the car door for her.

They stepped inside and were greeted by a server with a Sweet Shoppe t-shirt. "Hi, can I get you a table?"

"We're here to meet up with Julie." She glanced around the cute shop, her mouth watering at the enticing aromas.

"Oh, about the wedding cake. Congratulations to you two." The woman smiled warmly at them.

"What?" She shook her head violently. "No…" She shook her head again for emphasis. "No, it's not for… not for us."

"Oh, I just assumed…"

"We're just helping with some last-minute plans for our best friends," Scott countered smoothly, but he tossed a grin at her, obviously realizing how flustered she was. And enjoying it.

"I'll go get her. Why don't you sit at that table over there?"

Thankfully, she could sit across from Scott,

not beside him. He was still grinning at her, and she wanted to reach over and wipe it from his face.

Julie came out and greeted them. "I'm glad I could help you out. That's terrible about what happened to the bride."

"It is. But we're so grateful you can make the cake."

"I brought out two samples for you. A lemon cake and a chocolate cake. I made them to serve at the store today. But I can make others."

They took a bite of each. The lemon was nice. She was sure Christie would love it.

"I like the chocolate the best," Scott asserted.

"I don't think that's the best choice." She glared at him, then looked up at Julie. "But it's very good. I just don't think Christie wants chocolate."

"Chocolate is Tony's favorite." He eyed her.

"I could do a mix of flavors. A tiered cake," Julie suggested. "When I do that, I put a separator between the layers. Or I could do a separate groom's cake in chocolate."

"I think the lemon will be fine. It has such a delicate lemon flavor. It's wonderful." Not that she liked lemon cake, but Christie did, and that's what was important.

"And the groom's cake," Scott insisted.

"No, we don't need that." She pinned him with a hard stare, determined to win this argument.

"We do." He leaned back in his chair and crossed his arms.

Julie smothered a smile. "So… what's the verdict?"

She stared at Scott just sitting there with a determined look on his face. And to be honest, the groom's cake was a good idea. She just hated for him to be right. To give him that satisfaction. But that was on her. Not what was best for Christie and Tony. "We'll go with both."

"Great. Sounds good." Julie nodded.

"But white icing on the chocolate cake." So at least they'd look pretty sitting next to each other on the table.

Julie handed her a couple sheets of paper. "Here are pictures of some cakes I've decorated. Did you have a specific style in mind?"

She pointed to one of the photos. "This is nice. Simple. I think this will work." It was two-tiered with lacy icing around the edges.

81

"I could add a small bunch of flowers on top."

"Oh, could you do daisies? We're using them as flowers for the wedding."

"I'm sure Flossie's Flower Shop will have daisies. I'll double-check, but they usually do."

"Oh, that's where we're getting the flowers for the wedding. That would be perfect."

"Great. I'll ring up the order for you."

Julie walked away, and Scott took another bite of the chocolate cake. "This is way better than the lemon cake."

She rolled her eyes at him. "You're wrong."

"I'm right. And you don't like lemon cake. You just like to argue with me."

She glared at him. He was wrong, but there wasn't much use in arguing with him. He never thought he was wrong. And maybe, just maybe, he was right this time. She choked back a sigh.

Julie returned with the order written up. "I hope this helps. Did you get the rest of the wedding sorted out?"

Jill shook her head. "Not quite. There was a mix-up at the bridal salon and they ended up sending her dress to someone in Paris."

"Oh, no."

"Yeah, Christie is pretty upset. It was simple

and so her. I'm going to go out wedding dress shopping with her after we get back to Moonbeam."

The door to the shop opened and a woman with coppery red hair entered, waving to Julie.

"Hey, Charlotte. Be with you in a minute," Julie called out, then froze and snapped her fingers, her eyes widening. "I have an idea. Charlotte, come over here for a second."

Charlotte crossed over to them. "Hi."

"This is Jill and Scott. They're here picking out a wedding cake."

"Oh, congratulations," Charlotte smiled at them, her blue eyes twinkling. "Just got married a bit ago myself. Highly recommend it."

"No... we're not getting married," Jill quickly corrected her, then glared at Scott, who sat there grinning. His grin was the most annoying look ever.

"Their best friends are getting married over in Moonbeam. A mix-up happened and now they are planning the wedding in just a few days. The wedding is Sunday. Jill and Scott are just helping out."

"Oh, I see."

"Anyway... the bride is without a wedding

dress right now…" Julie looked at Charlotte, who broke into a wide smile.

"And you're thinking the same thing I am?" Charlotte asked.

"I am." Julie nodded.

Charlotte took out her phone and scrolled through it for a moment, then held it out for Jill to see. "This was my dress."

Jill looked at it. It was the perfect dress. Simple. Knee-length. Sleeveless with a touch of lace. "That's lovely. Where did you find it? I think Christie would love one just like that."

"Is she near my size?"

Jill looked at Charlotte for a moment. "Yes."

Julie laughed. "I swear that dress is magical."

"I'm confused…" Jill frowned, looking between Julie and Charlotte. She glanced at Scott, who just shrugged.

Julie sat down beside her. "You see… I wore that dress at my wedding. A friend of mine owns a vintage shop here and found that dress for me. It's very special. There's a note in the pocket from the original owner of the dress."

"I left the note in the pocket when I wore it," Charlotte added. "It was like a blessing from Barbara, the original bride."

"Anyway, Charlotte needed a wedding dress, so I gave it to her," Julie said.

"And now I could give it to Christie if she likes it. And Ruby—that's my mother-in-law—she could alter it for her if she needs it."

"This sounds almost too good to be true. Can you send me that photo so I can send it to Christie?"

Charlotte texted her a few photos of the dress, and Jill sent them off to Christie with a quick message. Within minutes she got back a text filled with exclamation points and grinning emojis saying Christie loved the dress.

"Well, I guess we have an answer." She sighed in relief.

"Let me call Ruby and see if we can set up a time this afternoon for Christie to try it on. That will give Ruby a few days to alter it if needed." Charlotte dialed her phone.

Jill set up an appointment for late afternoon and they headed out to Scott's car. A smug look landed on his face as he raced in front of her to open the car door for her with a flourish. She ignored him and ducked under his arm to get in.

They headed back to Moonbeam, this time with the windows up and the air-conditioning on because the day had begun to warm up. She stared out the window, her mind full of to-dos.

"I'm impressed you're pulling this all off." Scott interrupted her thoughts.

She turned to look at him. His eyes said he was sincere and almost looked like he *was* impressed. "It's the lists."

"Maybe. I think it's just more your pure force of will."

Was that a compliment? Or was he just saying she was stubborn? She really wasn't sure. This older Scott was a strange mix of annoyance and surprises.

CHAPTER 10

Violet grabbed her cell phone and a small wallet that held her license, credit card, and maybe twenty dollars. She wasn't much of a purse person. She shoved them in her pockets. Rob looked up from his computer. "You leaving?"

She'd hoped she might be able to just sneak out without him noticing, but no luck. "I'm headed to Sea Glass Cafe."

"Oh?"

She sighed. "Yes, I'm meeting Melody for ice cream."

"Ah, taking my advice to take a bit of time off." He grinned at her triumphantly. Exactly the expression she was trying to avoid.

"No, I just wanted some ice cream."

"Whatever you say, sis." He smirked and bent back over his laptop.

She ignored him, resisting the childish urge to stick her tongue out at him like she'd done when she was a kid. Turning her back on him, she crossed into the office, but not before seeing him glance up and grin again.

"Aspen, I won't be long. Just headed to town for a bit."

"Take as long as you like. I've got everything covered here. You deserve a nice long break."

What was up with everyone thinking she needed a break?

She headed out into the sunshine and down the street toward town. A perfect day for a walk. Warm, but not too warm. Sunny skies dotted with clouds. The kind of day that made her love Moonbeam so much. Maybe taking a break wasn't such a bad idea. But she'd never tell Rob that he was right. Ever. Any more than he'd ever admit she was right about something. Sibling rivalry was a real thing. Not that she didn't adore her brother. She did. They just both liked to be right.

She stepped into Sea Glass Cafe and waited a moment for her eyes to adjust from the bright sunlight to the inside lighting of the cafe. Only one table was filled with customers, and Melody waved to her from behind the ice cream counter. She headed over.

"I just finished my shift. Perfect timing. I'll make us some shakes and we can go sit at a table. I'll be glad to get off my feet. Came in early to help Evelyn cook, then worked the floor the rest of the day. Go on over and pick a table."

She sat at a table by the window and Melody joined her and set a large vanilla shake in front of her, sighing as she sat down across from her. "Ah, this feels great."

Violet dug a long spoon into the thick shake, took a bite, and got an immediate stab of a cold headache from the frosty concoction. "This is so good. I don't know how you can stand working here. Between Evelyn's cooking and the ice cream, I'd gain fifty pounds. At least."

Melody laughed. "Well, I'm rushing around all day, so I guess that helps."

"I've been busy, too, with this wedding coming up this weekend."

"The one where they had to plan everything themselves because of the missing wedding coordinator?"

"That's the one. I feel so sorry for the bride.

But her maid of honor, Jill, is a wonder. She's got almost everything set into place. I don't know how she did it."

"I don't know how you'd plan a wedding in less than a week."

"I don't know either, but it appears it can be done." She took another bite, waiting for the accompanying cold headache. Yep, there it was. "Jill was saying they were all around fifty. Jill, Christie, the groom, and the best man. Friends from high school. Christie and the groom had been friends all that time and then it became more. They realized their feelings for each other."

"That's wonderful."

"Gives me hope of finding someone, someday." Violet shrugged.

"Being married to the right person is so... wonderful," Melody whispered, sadness covering her expression.

"I'm sorry, Mel. All this talk of marriage. It must be hard for you."

Melody gave her a small smile. "No, it's fine. It's been two years now. You'd think I'd be used to being a widow. Anyway, I'm happy for people finding love. Getting married."

"You never talk about him."

"John? Most people get uncomfortable if I talk about him."

"I wouldn't."

Melody's eyes glistened as her sad look slowly turned into a wistful smile. "John was the most wonderful man. We talked about anything and everything. And his laugh… it would make anyone who heard it break into a smile. He sang all the time—off-key and messed up the words to songs—but it just made me happy. He brought little gifts for no reason. We were so happy. We were planning to have a family."

"I'm sorry. It must be so hard for you now."

"It is. I've kind of gotten used to being without him. But kind of not. I don't think I'll ever get over the loss of him. It was so sudden. Unexpected. So young to lose his life to cancer."

Violet couldn't even imagine what Melody had gone through. Such loss. She still mourned the loss of her parents, but that was more of a cycle of life—though so painful—and to be expected at some point. But losing a spouse so young? That was unexpected and horrible.

No wonder Ethan hadn't asked Melody out yet. It would be hard to compete with the memory of John. But she still hoped Melody would find love again someday.

"Anyway, enough talk of this," Melody said. "The Jenkins twins came in today with some fresh gossip."

She grinned. "And?" Jackie and Jillian Jenkins always knew the news first. And weren't afraid to share. With *everyone*.

Melody regaled her with the newest town gossip as they sat and enjoyed their shakes. She was glad she and Melody had become friends. She was easy to talk to, and it was nice to have a friend in town. She'd moved around a lot and hadn't made many close friends. She'd always been jealous of women talking about their best friends or close group of friends. She'd never had that.

Maybe she'd find that in Moonbeam.

CHAPTER 11

That afternoon, Jill and Christie went back to Belle Island. Ruby greeted them when they arrived. "I'm so pleased to be able to help you."

Ruby held up the dress, and Christie's eyes filled with tears. "Oh, it's even more beautiful in person."

"Go try it on. Use the bedroom down the hall."

Christie returned, her eyes shining, a trembling smile on her face. "Oh, Jill. Isn't it just perfect?"

"You look beautiful." The dress did suit Christie.

Ruby looked it over carefully. "I think I need to take it in a little here. But otherwise, I think it

93

will work perfectly. And Jill is right. You look beautiful in it."

"I can't believe how this worked out." Christie stood in front of the mirror, an awed expression on her face. "I love this one more than the first one I picked out. It all worked out for the best."

"I think there's a bit of magic with this dress. It always seems to show up at just the right time, for just the right person." Ruby stepped back. "Yes, it's perfect for you."

Christie changed out of the dress, thanked Ruby, and made plans to come back on Saturday morning to get it.

They walked outside to the car. "Ruby's just lovely, isn't she? So friendly and she's so nice to fit in the alterations at the last minute." Christie paused by the car door when her phone dinged. "Oh, it's Tony. He says he and Scott are headed over here to the island and want us to meet them at a place called Magic Cafe for an early dinner." She looked up. "Is that okay with you?"

Well, it wasn't, but she couldn't actually say no. She'd planned on eating alone tonight. Despite her wishes, she put on a wide, enthusiastic smile. She was getting good at these fake enthusiastic smiles. "Yes, that's great."

They got in the car and she looked up directions. Not far. She headed over to the restaurant. They were greeted by an older woman with a welcoming smile. "Hi. Welcome to Magic Cafe. A table for two?"

"No, we'll have two more. I think they're just a few minutes behind us," Christie said.

"Is this your first time here?"

"It is," Jill answered.

"Well, I'm very glad you came. I'm Tally, by the way. The owner. Always love for new people to discover the cafe. Follow me. I'll give you a table right by the beach."

Jill swept her gaze around the charming cafe as they made their way outside. Tables were scattered around a large deck at the edge of the beach. Ceiling fans swirled in lazy circles above the tables. "Oh, this is lovely."

"Thank you." Tally smiled in appreciation. "It is my happy place here on Belle Island. So, are you two staying here on the island?"

"No, we're over in Moonbeam at Blue Heron Cottages. We came over to meet with Ruby. She's altering a wedding dress for me."

Tally grinned. "Oh, you must be the bride whose coordinator let you down. And you're wearing Julie and Charlotte's dress."

Jill's mouth dropped open. "How do you know all that?"

Tally laughed. "It's a small island. Word gets around. And I'm sure that wedding dress will bring good luck and happiness to your marriage. It sure has for Julie and Charlotte."

Christie beamed. "I loved the dress."

Just then, Scott and Tony arrived and joined them at the table. Introductions were made, and Tally left to go get their drinks.

"This place is nice. I like that it's right on the beach." Tony settled onto the chair next to Christie.

Scott took one look at the empty chair next to Jill, grinned, and sat down beside her. Their drinks arrived, and they ordered—all of them choosing grouper and hushpuppies—and Jill concentrated on her drink and the view, not Scott whose knee kept bumping hers under the table. Maybe deliberately, if his grin was any indication.

"Hey, remember that time we all went to the river on that float trip?" Tony asked.

"The one where the girls insisted they were going to take their own canoe, so we took ours?" Scott laughed.

"We were doing fine for most of the day," Christie protested.

"Until you flipped the canoe. Lost one of your paddles—Jill's, I believe—and the cooler with all our food and drinks went floating down the river." Scott chuckled.

What was so funny about their canoe flipping? She hadn't been amused. They'd gotten soaked, and the water was *cold*. She'd lost a shoe. And her favorite pair of sunglasses. Not to mention all the teasing the guys had done for days and days after the trip.

"Right, and you guys were more interested in saving the cooler than helping us." She glared at Scott, just thinking of how annoyed she'd been.

"You were in your I-can-do-anything phase. Though come to think of it, you're always in that phase." Scott sent her a lazy grin.

Grin. Was that the only expression he had?

"Well, Scott was more interested in the cooler. I jumped out to help you two and get you to shore," Tony insisted.

"And that was the last float trip we ever took together." Christie shook her head. "But we did go camping that summer, too."

"We did. No big fiascos with that." Tony draped his arm around Christie's shoulder.

"If I remember correctly, someone kept saying he heard a bear or a coyote or something. Just trying to scare us." She raised an eyebrow and looked at Scott.

"And you were scared and agreed to share our tent with us. It worked." Scott winked.

Was a wink better or worse than his grin?

"No, but really. We had some great times." Christie and Tony shared a glance that connected the two, wrapped them in their own private cocoon.

Jill suddenly felt alone, even sitting here at the table with her friends. No, wait. Scott wasn't her friend. Not anymore.

"We had some good times," Scott said softly.

She turned her gaze from the happy couple to Scott. Okay, maybe they had. She remembered moonlight walks with Scott. Hours spent talking. And picnics at her favorite park. Going to the movies as soon as a blockbuster hit would come out. Dinners at Antonio's Cantina. Those days had been filled with friendship and laughter.

And kisses. Scott's kisses. She remembered

those. The way her heart would flutter when he glanced at her from across the room.

He leaned closer and whispered, "You're staring at me again."

Was she? "I… I was just thinking."

"Your cheeks are flushed."

"It's warm," she countered, unwilling to believe those memories had caused her to blush.

"We did have some good times. You and me," he said softly again.

She glanced across the table. Christie and Tony were so engrossed in each other they weren't paying any attention to her and Scott. She looked at Scott. "I guess we did have some good times."

He leaned back. "Never thought I'd hear you admit it."

What did the man want from her? Hadn't she just agreed with him? And that didn't happen very often.

Their food arrived, and it saved her from her memories. At least until they finished eating and Christie decided to ride back to Moonbeam with Tony and suggest that Scott ride back with her.

It was a never-ending drive back to

Moonbeam, no matter what the clock in the car said.

And still, Scott kept glancing over at her with that easy grin. Which she totally ignored. Totally.

CHAPTER 12

The next day, Violet was torn. She hated asking Rob for a favor. But the Bodines were throwing a surprise birthday party for Aspen this afternoon. Walker told her that Aspen had never had a birthday party. Ever. How was that possible?

She and Rob had yearly parties growing up. Such fun. And he'd visited for her fortieth birthday, even though she'd insisted she was just ignoring the day. He'd taken her out for a fancy dinner and gotten her a silver bracelet she adored.

But Rob had done so much for her here at the cottages. She hated asking him to run the office for her for a few hours while she went to the party.

Rose came into the office, took one look at her, and said, "You look upset. Confused? Something."

"I'm torn and don't know what I'm going to do. The Bodines are having a surprise birthday party for Aspen. But I can't really leave. I could ask Rob, but he's already done so much for me. I have two more cottages checking in for the wedding. Then we'll be full."

"Let me watch the desk for you."

"I couldn't ask you to do that."

"You didn't. I offered. I'd love to. You tell me which cottages you want people to be checked into and I'll handle it from there."

"Are you certain you want to do that? We're sure putting you to work around here. First the flowers. Then working the desk."

"I love feeling needed. I want to do this for you. Please let me." Rose's expression said she meant it.

"If you're sure." What a relief. She hated to miss Aspen's very first birthday party.

"What time do you need me?"

"I should leave in about an hour."

"I'll be back. You go and enjoy yourself. And I'll enjoy feeling useful. A win for both of us. I love being here at the cottages, but I'm used to being busy. I've explored the town. Walked the beach. Found a lovely bookstore and read a stack of books."

"Beachside Bookshop? Collette owns that. It's a wonderful shop, isn't it? She has a wealth of knowledge about all things books. She always has great recommendations for me. And did you know she has cookies and sweet tea every Saturday at the shop?"

"I should drop by on a Saturday then." Rose's eyes crinkled with amusement. "But probably not this one. I'll have my hands full with the flower arrangements."

"I'll be glad to help you with those, although I know nothing about arranging flowers. I could at least be your gopher or something."

"I promise I'll ask if I need any help."

"This is perfect. Thank you. I'll see you in an hour."

Her guilt at missing Aspen's first birthday party slipped away. She was glad she'd already picked up a present. A lovely lightweight sweater in a peach color that she thought would look great on her.

She glanced at her watch. An hour to get

some work done, then she'd head to the Bodines' place. She'd never been there but heard it was a lovely old house right on the bay. She couldn't wait to see it. Being invited to the party made her feel like she'd become more of a real resident of the town. That she belonged. And she liked that feeling.

Aspen knew she should probably be used to being around the Bodines by now. She was dating Walker. She worked with his parents, Jimmy and Sally, at the restaurant, along with his sister, Tara. So why was she nervous about going to their home for a barbecue today?

She'd changed clothes three times—or was it four—trying to look casual but put together. She couldn't wear the exact same dress she'd borrowed from her sister the last time she went to the Bodines'. She finally decided on a simple short-sleeved, white button-up blouse and a pair of navy capri slacks. That was the best she could do.

After she had a bit of savings put aside, she was going to take herself shopping for a few more outfits, so she felt like she fit in better with the Bodines. Though that was probably on her. Her feelings. They never acted like she didn't fit in with them.

With one last look in the mirror, she still felt... plain. Then she remembered a necklace Willow had given her, made out of brightly colored beads. She slipped that on. There, that looked better.

She went out to the porch, waiting for Walker. He insisted on picking her up even though she'd told him she could just walk. Pacing back and forth on the porch, she again wondered if she'd chosen the right outfit. Maybe a dress would be better? But Walker said it was casual. Did that mean casual like a sundress to the Bodines?

And why was she so nervous? They had been nothing but warm and welcoming to her. Honestly, they treated her almost like family. Well, what she assumed it would feel like to be treated like family. She'd never really experienced that. But she'd dreamed about it.

But she had a family now, she reminded herself. She had her sister, Willow. And Willow had promised to come back to Moonbeam and visit soon.

Walker drove up, and it was too late to

change her mind about her outfit. She put on a brave smile and walked over to his car. He jumped out and gave her a quick kiss. "You look great."

"Thanks." Those were exactly the words she needed to hear. "You look great, too."

He looked unbelievably handsome in khaki shorts, a collared knit shirt that stretched across his broad shoulders, and leather sandals. But then he looked handsome in whatever he wore.

"Come on. We've got a barbecue to get to." He held open the car door, and she climbed inside.

They pulled into the drive at the Bodines' and she took a deep breath. She could do this. She could. Walker had assured her it was just a little barbecue. He said his family had them all the time for any occasion or no occasion at all.

He held her hand—and she might have grasped it just a bit too tightly—as they walked through the gate to the backyard. They crossed into the yard and she stopped, looking around in surprise. A huge happy birthday banner stretched between two palm trees. A large table was overflowing with food and... was that a birthday cake complete with candles?

"Surprise!" everyone called out.

"Happy birthday, Aspen." Walker's mouth curved into a smile of satisfaction.

"All this is for me? But... but how did you know?" she whispered.

His eyes twinkled with satisfaction that he'd pulled off his surprise. "Hey, your birthdate was on the forms you filled out to work at Jimmy's. My family is not one to let a birthday go by unnoticed."

Tears threatened to spill as emotions overwhelmed her. "Oh, Walker... this is the most wonderful thing anyone has ever done for me." She glanced around at the crowd of people. All the Bodines. Violet. Melody from Sea Glass Cafe. Some workers from Jimmy's. So many people.

He laughed and kissed her forehead. "Come on. Come enjoy the party."

He led her over to Sally, who gave her a hug. "I wasn't sure we'd pull off the surprise."

Tara walked up. "No kidding. Walker couldn't stop pestering us about all the details. I was sure you were going to overhear us talking at Jimmy's."

"I didn't hear a thing."

"You certainly looked surprised." Walker's dad came over. "Nothing I like better than a surprise party that's actually a surprise. Hard to keep a secret with this family."

"I can't believe you guys did all of this for me."

"Can't let a birthday go by uncelebrated in this family." Tara laughed and tugged her hand. "Come on, let's go open your presents. Look at that haul."

She stared over at a table laden with brightly wrapped presents. Joy bubbled up inside her and she fought to keep back tears. "I don't even know what to say. This is all so... so much. So wonderful."

"Hey, that's what happens when the Bodine family takes a liking to you." Walker nodded toward the table of gifts. "Let's go see what you got."

"Burgers will be ready in about twenty minutes," Jimmy said, standing by the grill and waving a spatula for emphasis. "Go open the gifts."

"And Mom outdid herself on that cake. Vanilla with a strawberry cream inside," Tara added. "Though she had to keep chasing Walker away so he wouldn't cut into it early."

"Hey, I need my nourishment."

She smiled at the two siblings and their constant easygoing teasing. They headed over to the table and she stood in front of it, staring. So many gifts. She'd never seen so many gifts before. Not for her, anyway.

Tara bumped her softly with her hip. "Go on."

She opened the gifts, overwhelmed at everyone's generosity. Things for her cottage. Clothes. New clothes! She was so delighted.

She ate way too much food, danced to the music spilling from the speakers set by the back deck, and laughed and talked and had the best time. All this for her. She couldn't get over it.

Afterward, Walker drove her home, his car piled with gifts. When they got back to her cottage, he hauled her presents inside. Then they sat out on her porch, side by side on the porch swing Violet had found in the shed and Walker had hung for her a few days ago.

"I had the best day ever." She leaned against Walker as he pulled her close against his side.

"That's what I was hoping for."

"I can't believe you did all that for me."

"Of course we did. We all love you," he

said, his expression tender and his eyes filled with intensity and emotion.

"You what?" Her voice squeaked and her pulse pounded so loud in her ears she was certain she'd heard wrong.

He tilted her chin up and locked his eyes with hers. "I love you," he said softly as he brushed a lock of hair away from her face, then trailed a finger along her jawline.

Her heart swelled and her pulse raced. "Oh…" was all she could think to say, and she thought she was doing well to get that one word out.

He leaned down and kissed her gently— twice—then pulled back slightly. "You've brought so much happiness into my life. I can't imagine my life without you in it."

"But it hasn't been that long that we've known each other." Images of all the time they'd spent together the last few weeks flickered through her mind.

"Doesn't matter. I know how my heart feels. And it's telling me I love you."

She looked up into his eyes, wondering if she dared to tell him how she felt. Loving people hadn't turned out very well for her in her lifetime. Yet, she knew how her heart felt, too. There was no denying it.

"I love you, too, Walker."

And he kissed her again. This time long and thoroughly until it left her breathless.

CHAPTER 13

Jill sat at the table in the cottage with Christie going over the expansive perfect wedding to-do list she'd found online. She had to make sure she hadn't forgotten some detail that needed to be attended to.

"Take a break," Christie insisted. "You've been working nonstop to pull off this wedding."

"I just want to make sure I didn't forget anything."

"Anything that's forgotten will just have to be forgotten. I don't care. I'm going to have a wedding on Sunday and that's all that matters."

"I want it to be perfect."

"It will be. I'm marrying Tony after all these years. My family and friends are here. You found me the perfect dress. You even found food and flowers. And this wedding is more *me* than the one we paid good money for the wedding coordinator to plan."

"You're really fine with all the arrangements?"

"I'm more than fine. I love everything."

She let out a long breath. "I hope so."

Christie stood. "Do you mind if Tony and I sneak away for dinner? I'd love some time alone with him."

"Not at all. Go have some couple time." And that way, she wouldn't have to worry about having dinner with Scott yet again.

"Okay, I'm going to go change." Christie headed back to her bedroom.

A knock sounded and Jill went to answer the door. Surprise washed through her at seeing Scott standing there.

"Hey, I heard that Tony and Christie want to go to dinner, just the two of them. I thought that maybe you and I could go grab something to eat."

"The two of us?"

He nodded. "You have to eat, right?"

"I'm not very hungry." Her stomach took that exact moment to growl and rumble, highlighting her lie.

He cocked an eyebrow. "Oh?"

She let out a long sigh. "Okay, I'm hungry."

"So, that's a yes?"

"That's a yes."

"Perfect. It's a date. I'll come over and pick you up in about half an hour." He loped back to his cottage, but not before sending her a satisfied grin.

That grin of his. Again.

And it was *not* a date.

Christie walked back into the front room dressed in a floral sundress, her hair brushed and floating gently around her shoulders, her makeup refreshed.

"You look nice."

"Thanks. I'm really looking forward to some alone time with Tony. I feel like every moment has been filled with plans and rushing around."

"You're right to take some time for just the two of you."

"Do you want me to bring you back something to eat?" Christie glanced in the mirror and tucked a lock of her hair back behind one ear.

"Ah… no. I'm going to grab something to eat with Scott."

Christie turned around, her eyes wide, a

smile creeping onto her lips. "Really? That's great."

She frowned. "I don't know what's great about it."

"I just meant… well, I'm glad you two are getting along. What are you going to wear?"

She looked down at her shorts and t-shirt. "This?"

"No, you're not." Christie's eyebrows rose. "You need to change."

"This is fine. Everything is casual down here. I'm sure we're not going anywhere fancy."

"Go put on that teal sundress you brought. That's a great color for you."

"I was going to wear that Saturday for the rehearsal."

"Then what else do you have to wear?" Christie grabbed her hand and tugged her back toward the bedrooms. "Let's have a look."

Christie looked through the clothes hanging in the closet and pulled out a simple knit skirt and a pink top. "Wear this." Christie shoved the clothes into her arms, started to walk out of the room, and called back over her shoulder, "And those pink sandals."

She figured it was wrong to argue with a bride, so she put on the outfit. It did hit the right vibe for her. Casual but put together. That worked. She put on a touch of eyeshadow, mascara, and lipstick, though she wasn't sure why. Who was she trying to impress?

But she was years older than when she and Scott had dated. She wondered what he thought about her looks now. He'd gotten even more attractive as he aged in that aggravating way that some men had.

Christie poked her head in the room. "I'm leaving now. You two have a good time. I'll see you later."

"Okay, have fun." But she wasn't really looking to have a good time herself. She was just going to have dinner. That was it.

She looked in the mirror, trying to decide what to do with her hair. Scott used to say he loved her hair down, loose around her shoulders. But she felt more confident with it twisted back in a tight, precise bun. As a compromise, she pulled it back into a loose knot. With one last look in the mirror, she headed out to the front room, pacing back and forth, waiting.

117

After Tony left, Scott changed clothes and paced the cottage, waiting for half an hour to pass. Jill surprised him by saying yes to dinner. He'd actually asked her just to get a rise out of her and hear a long list of all the reasons she wouldn't go with him. He'd expected to see those familiar bright pink spots on her cheeks and blazing eyes as she shot him down.

But she said yes.

And that surprised him.

But it pleased him.

Maybe they'd have time to talk. Really talk. And he could get to know this older version of the Jill he once knew. This older version of the younger Jill whose heart he'd broken.

But that wasn't really his fault. It was just something he had to do. For her sake. And it had crushed his heart, his soul, when he did it. Even as he was shattering hers. But it had been for the best. Or at least he'd thought so at the time.

He shoved those thoughts away and popped back to his thoughts on *this* Jill. This fifty-year-old Jill. Well, almost fifty. Her birthday was Sunday. He should get her a little gift, right? Then again, she was probably one of those women who ignored their birthdays on the big milestone ones.

Though, to be honest, she was more beautiful now than when they were younger. She had a few wrinkles around her eyes. He wasn't sure you could call them smile lines because Jill was always so intense. Maybe they were tension lines. Her hair didn't have one strand of gray, but you never knew with women. Maybe she dyed it. But it was still the same color as when she was young. A shiny chestnut brown. She had put on a few pounds, but not many, just enough for soft curves. And her honey-brown eyes still flashed when he teased and exasperated her, which he loved to do.

What could he get her for her birthday? He was at a loss. He'd done great for her sixteenth birthday, all those years ago. He'd found her a necklace with a rose quartz heart. She'd been delighted with it. Said it was perfect. She wore it every day until... until he broke up with her. She ripped off the necklace and threw it at him, tears streaming down her cheeks, then turned and walked away from him, sobbing.

He'd stood there, his heart crumbling, his breath caught in his throat, choking him. He wanted to reach out and stop her. Tell her it had been a mistake. Comfort her. Comfort him. Stop the stabbing ache in his heart.

But he hadn't.

Instead, he dropped to his knees and searched the surrounding grass until he found the necklace. He still had it, which was silly. But sometimes, in weak moments, he took it out and just held it up to the light, wondering what his life would have been like if he'd followed his heart that day instead of logic. Logic that said ending their relationship was the right thing to do. Sensible.

But oh so painful.

Pushing the memories aside, he leafed through the booklet on the table, listing places to eat around town. Where to take her? Jimmy's had been great, with a fantastic view. But she'd probably want to go somewhere new. There was a Sea Glass Cafe in town. Or a Portside Grill out on the wharf that looked like it might be nice. He'd take her there. She probably liked fancy these days.

He glanced at his watch. Finally, time to go get her. He left his cottage, whistling under his breath.

She opened the door to his knock, and he stood there like a fool, just staring at her. She honestly took his breath away, just like she used to. Her bright pink blouse perfectly matched the two bright spots on her cheeks as she shifted from foot to foot and nervously smoothed her palms along her hips.

He cleared his throat. "Ah... are you ready?"

She nodded.

"I thought we'd go to Portside Grill. It's on the wharf."

"Sounds good."

She followed him out to his car, this time not arguing about who was going to drive. He opened the car door, and she slid inside, her skirt swishing against her long legs. Not that he was staring at her legs.

Only he was. He swallowed again. He'd thought he was way past the point where she had any effect on him. But he was wrong. He was in trouble. A lot of trouble.

CHAPTER 14

Jill was in trouble. A lot of trouble. Scott sucked all the oxygen out of her when he stood at the door. Her heart skipped a beat.

His bright blue shirt was the perfect match to the skies above them and highlighted his ocean blue eyes. She'd been immediately annoyed with herself for letting him get this type of reaction from her. So she'd ignored her reaction. Shoved it away.

Except when she followed him to his car and saw his long, tanned legs and broad shoulders and easygoing stride. Why was he so at ease? Why?

She obviously had no effect on him these days. Not like she used to. His eyes used to light up when he saw her with a look of delight and… love. They had been so in love. Or so she thought.

She silently arranged her skirt around her knees as she sat in his car, wondering how she was going to get through this evening and why she'd ever said yes to this really bad idea.

They got to the wharf, and she climbed awkwardly out of his car, ignoring his offered hand. There was no way she was taking his hand. She was rewarded for her decision with a slight stumble as she got out. Lovely. How did some women slide so gracefully out of cars?

They entered the wharf beneath its large, weathered sign and were soon caught up in the rather large crowd. A candy store caught her eye with a large sign proclaiming to have the best saltwater taffy in the state.

"We should stop and get you some on our way out." Scott nodded toward the shop. "You love saltwater taffy."

She did, but how did he remember that? He'd once driven hours in the snow to Estes Park to pick up taffy and surprise her. He used to always do special things like that. "Maybe," was all she answered, but her mouth watered at the thought.

They got to Portside Grill and stepped inside. As her eyes adjusted to the dimness, she grabbed his arm. And promptly let it go. "We can't eat here."

"Why not?"

"Because Christie and Tony are here. They want time alone, not us sitting at a nearby table."

"You're right. We'll find someplace else." They snuck back out of the restaurant.

"We could go back to Jimmy's at the end of the wharf. The food was good there." And it looked like they might have another fabulous sunset. She was kind of getting into the whole sunset thing.

"I didn't think you'd want to go back there again."

"No, it's fine. Let's do that." They headed to the end of the wharf. They were greeted by a woman they'd met last time. What was her name? Terry? Tawnya? No, Tara, that was it.

"Welcome back," she greeted them.

"Hi, Tara," she said triumphantly, pleased she'd remembered her name.

"Just two this time?"

She nodded. Yes, just two. At least that meant Scott would sit across from her instead of beside her, bumping into her. Though it also meant he'd be across from her and she'd have to look directly at him all evening.

They sat at their table, ordered drinks, and looked over the menu. She slowly read every single word of description on every single item on the menu.

Scott chuckled. "You about got that menu all memorized?"

She glared at him. "I was just making sure I was picking the right thing tonight."

"It's not a life-or-death decision. Just pick something that sounds good. I'm going for grouper again. I swear this area of Florida has the best grouper."

Grouper did sound good, but she didn't really want to give him the satisfaction of ordering what he suggested. She ordered a platter of shrimp and a small side salad.

They struggled with conversation during the meal with Scott trying to keep it going with questions and her giving one- or two-word answers. He finally set his fork down.

"What gives? I thought we were getting along okay. Now you're barely speaking to me."

Because she was nervous. Nervous to let him

in. Let him know her. Afraid that if she did, her heart might shatter again.

Where had those thoughts come from?

"I don't know what you're talking about," she lied.

"Sure you do." He wouldn't let her get away with her lie. He knew her too well.

She sucked in a deep breath. "Look, we can be friends—or at least friendly—for this wedding. I can do that. But I don't trust you. I don't want to get close to you. I'll never let you close enough to hurt me again."

A direct hit. Pain flashed through his eyes. "Jill, I am sorry. Sorry I hurt you."

"You... you shattered me. It was the last thing I expected. I know it was hard being so far apart after I went to college, but I thought we were stronger than the distance."

"You had everything ahead of you, though. A future with a fancy degree from Wharton. The world was yours for the asking."

She frowned. "But I wanted you in that world."

"I was getting a two-year degree from college with no plans to ever leave Sweet River. And there isn't much need for a fancy MBA in Sweet River, now is there?"

"We could have worked that out."

"I wasn't going to hold you back. Look at you now with your hotshot job. Christie told me all about it. And you're close to another promotion. See, it worked out how it was supposed to."

She eyed him. "Did it?" The hurt and pain from their breakup all those years ago threatened to crash over her. Again. She steeled herself against it. Ignored it.

"It did." He nodded.

He wasn't about to tell her the rest of it. The whole truth. This would just have to do.

He couldn't bear to tell her about that conversation with her father. The one where her father said to stay away from Jill. Let her get her degree and move on. Insisting that there was no future for Jill in Sweet River Falls.

Then Mr. Sawyer made vague threats about talking to his best friend, Old Man Dobbs, and making it difficult for Scott's mother to find a new job. She'd just lost her job when a small store had closed in town. Dobbs held a lot of power in their small town, and Scott had no doubt that if he spread the word not to hire his mother, she'd have a very hard time finding a new job.

Jill and her father had been really close back then. He couldn't exactly tell her what her father had said to him. He wasn't even sure if she'd believe him.

And part of him agreed with the man. There wasn't much of a future for Jill in Sweet River. And he had no plans to leave. It had just been him and his mother since the day his father left and he and his mom had pulled up stakes and landed in Sweet River Falls.

She'd worked so hard to support them both. Long hours. Making sure he still had some extras, like equipment to play the sports he loved. She'd have no one if he left Sweet River. And he couldn't do that after all she'd done for him.

So, he'd done as Mr. Sawyer had asked. He broke up with Jill. That night after they broke up, he went home with the quartz heart clutched in his hand.

His mom had taken one look at him and asked him what was wrong. When he told her he'd just broken up with Jill, she pinned him with a hard look and asked why he'd done such a fool thing as that. But he hadn't explained any more to her.

Then he started to date someone new. She was funny and vivacious—if a bit self-centered—but just the thing he needed to distract himself.

What a mistake that had been. But he'd paid the price for that mistake.

He dragged his thoughts from the past and looked across the table at Jill, who was staring out at the sunset, the warm glow illuminating her hair. She really was beautiful. He almost said that aloud. But he caught himself just in time, keeping this thought to himself.

He reached across the table and covered her hand. She quickly whipped her face around to stare at him.

"I am very sorry I hurt you. I am. I regret that to this day. I don't expect you to ever forgive me, but just know that I'm sorry."

She stared down at his hand covering hers, then back up to lock eyes with his. "I never understood why. I loved you so much."

"Ah, Jillybean." His heart squeezed in his chest, breaking all over again. But he couldn't tell her that he'd loved her, too, and that's why he'd done what he did.

And he certainly couldn't tell her he loved her still. To this very day. To this very moment. No, he couldn't tell her that.

CHAPTER 15

Jill walked beside Scott along the wharf after a dinner that was surprisingly pleasant, even with their rather serious discussion. It was kind of a relief to just get that out in the open.

Scott stopped short by the taffy shop. "Seriously, I'm going to buy you a box a taffy. You know you want it."

She did. A lot. "Okay, but only because you're insisting."

He grinned. "Then I'm insisting." He held the door open for her.

They walked inside, and the aroma of cooked sugar, mint, and caramel swirled around her. Even though she'd eaten a good-sized meal, her mouth watered in anticipation.

"Vanilla, right? Your favorite. And mint. And cinnamon."

He remembered her three favorites. "Yes, that's right."

He ordered a box and handed it to her as they walked out. "Go ahead. You know you want some."

She opened the box and took out a piece of vanilla, unwrapping it and popping it into her mouth. The sweet vanilla assaulted her taste buds. So delicious.

He laughed. "Knew you'd choose vanilla first."

"Want one?" She held out the box, and he took a mint one.

"There are some benches out by the marina. Want to sit there for a bit and people watch?"

That sounded like fun. Relaxing. They used to love to people watch and make up stories about the strangers who walked past them. "Sure, we could sit for a while."

They found a bench and both took another piece of taffy. "This is so good. I hope I don't eat the entire box in like a day." She closed the lid, trying to ignore that it was calling for her to have just one more piece.

"There's more where that came from. I could go buy another box."

"You will not. This is more than enough."

"It's good... but not as good as the Estes Park taffy, is it?"

"Not quite," she admitted. She should go back there the next time she went home to Sweet River.

And that thought surprised her. That she was considering visiting Sweet River Falls. And that she had thought of it as *home*.

"So, do you like still living in Sweet River?" she asked.

"I do. Have my own place now out on the Lone Elk Lake."

"You do?" She couldn't quite picture that. Those cabins didn't come cheap, and he'd always been so laid back about saving money. As in, he never had any saved.

"Why do you look so surprised?"

"I don't know. I just don't picture you with a home to take care of. Doing yard work. Stuff like that."

"I actually love puttering in the yard. I grow some veggies in pots during the summer. I don't even mind all the snow shoveling. Well, usually.

Last year we got dumped on week after week. I was ready for spring."

She hadn't picked up a snow shovel in years. Her condo complex always shoveled the sidewalks, and she had a parking space in the garage. And the snow in the city was dingy and gray, not white and pretty like the snowfalls in Sweet River.

"So Christie said you have a condo, not a house." Scott stretched out his long legs and put his arms up, lacing his fingers behind his head.

"Yes. A condo. I don't have time to keep up a house." She just called maintenance if there was ever a problem and they'd come in and deal with it. And she didn't even have a plant to take care of in her condo. She'd tried. Twice. And both times the plant had died because she'd forgotten about it. So she decided she didn't want to be a plant killer and gave up on them.

"So, what do you do when you're not working?"

She shrugged. "Sleep? I'm always working, it seems."

"Even the weekends?"

"Usually."

"Doesn't sound like a great way to live."

"Thanks so much for your opinion," she snapped.

"No." He took his arms down and touched her hand. "I didn't mean that. I just mean... well, it's good to take time for yourself."

"I enjoy working," she insisted. And she did. Even though there was a nagging thought in the back of her mind that she was burned out and he was kind of right. Not that she'd admit that to him. She'd focused so long on this next promotion that she hadn't taken time to think about much else.

"Whatever makes you happy." He shifted his leg and bumped against hers. She jerked her leg away as if she'd been touched by fire.

She was happy, wasn't she? A good job. A nice condo. Money to buy what she wanted, not that she bought a lot. Once her condo was furnished and she had a reliable car, what else did she need? Oh, and proper work clothes. Those were important.

"Are you happy?" He searched her face.

"I... I am." Maybe there had been some discontent creeping around the edges of her life for the last few years. But she'd never taken much time to examine those thoughts.

"Do you travel? Take vacations?"

"Not often. I travel for work some. But not really for vacations."

He cocked his head. "So, when was the last time you took time off before this week for Christie's wedding?"

She frowned and thought for a moment. "Last summer?" No, that wasn't right. It was the summer before that. She'd gone to the shore for a long weekend with a couple of work colleagues. Thinking back on it, though, they'd talked work all weekend.

He raised his eyebrows and shook his head slightly.

She changed the subject. "And how about you? What are you doing now? Workwise, I mean."

"I own a guide company in Sweet River. We do guided hiking to some of the Fourteeners." He looked at her. "You remember. The mountains in Colorado that are over fourteen thousand feet. Fifty-eight of them."

She nodded, vaguely remembering discussion about them. She hadn't been much of an avid hiker like so many people in Sweet River.

"We do some guided backpacking to the backcountry. We have fishing guides."

"I had no idea you had a company like that."

"We were written up in The Denver Post as one of the top five guide companies in the state. Business has been booming." His eyes shone with pride. "I really enjoy it. As it's grown, I spend more time in the office, but I love it when I can get out and be one of the guides."

That he owned his own successful business astonished her. How did he get to that point with his laid-back attitude, lack of planning... and the fact that he never, ever made a list? But it was obvious he was proud of his company, his success. Why had Christie never told her about this?

Oh yeah, because they had an unwritten rule to never talk about Scott. Ever.

"That's so great that you do that. Own that company, I mean. You always loved being outdoors."

"I do. And I remember trying to make a hiker out of you." A smile tugged at the corners of his mouth.

"You got me up on Castlewood Peak and there was a ridiculously skinny trail we were supposed to climb. The drop-off over the edge looked like it was miles down."

"I told you I wouldn't let you fall."

But she hadn't believed him, and they'd turned back. After that, it was some easy day hikes for picnics, but he did his harder hikes with friends. There were times she wished she had trusted him, taken that short section of the path because the photos she'd seen of the view from the top of Castlewood Peak were breathtaking. But she just couldn't make herself do it.

"You were so disappointed in me," she looked at him, watching his face closely.

"No, I was disappointed that you didn't trust me enough. Didn't believe me when I said it would be okay. I really wanted to show you the view. We were so close and only had that short ledge to travel."

"I guess we got close to a lot of things in our relationship but never hit the peak, did we?"

His look said he understood her double meaning as sadness crept across his eyes.

"And I trusted you with my heart… and look what that got me." Another direct hit. It just slipped out.

His eyes filled with pain. "I'll keep repeating how sorry I am until you believe me."

"Sometimes sorry isn't enough, though, is it?"

"It won't stop me from trying."

She stood up from the bench and grabbed the box of taffy. Too much serious talk. Too many painful memories. "We should go. It's getting late."

He sat there for a moment, staring up at her, then pushed off the bench. "Yes, it's getting late." He gave her a look so full of sadness, regret, and longing it nearly took her breath away.

Her heart squeezed, and she sucked in a quick breath. That looked etched itself in her mind, and she was certain she wouldn't forget it for a long, long time.

CHAPTER 16

Jill snuck out of the cottage early on Friday, letting Christie sleep in. Christie had gotten in late last night, and Jill pretended to be asleep in her room instead of going out to chat with her. Christie would have pummeled her with questions about going out to dinner with Scott, and she wasn't ready to have that discussion.

She walked out into the early morning air with the humidity clinging to the slight breeze. It was supposed to be another hot day, but a cool front was expected for tomorrow, which would be nice. It was predicted to drop the temperature ten degrees for the wedding on Sunday. That would be perfect.

She headed down to the beach. A few of the

last stars were hanging around, fighting to hold their place as the sky brightened. As she reached the beach, she saw Rose sitting near the shoreline. Rose waved, and she headed toward her.

"Come join me." Rose patted the sand beside her. "I try to catch the sunrise most mornings."

"The sky here in Moonbeam is so magical." She dropped down beside Rose and crossed her legs. "And the sunsets are so full of color. More brilliant than I've ever seen." Or more likely, it was because she rarely stopped to catch a sunset, let it hit her consciousness.

"Yes, the sunsets here are wonderful, too. The sunrises on the East Coast are nice, but I prefer our slight sunrises reflected in the clouds and on the water, then the spectacular sunsets over the gulf."

They sat quietly while the sky brightened and the sun painted the clouds a pale pink. It was so peaceful, just sitting here and doing nothing. She tugged in a breath of the salt-tinged air, letting it soak through her and bring a peace she rarely felt.

"So, I saw you leave with that young fellow

last night. The one staying with the groom. Did you have a nice time?"

The peace disintegrated, crumbling into sharp, jagged pieces. "Ah… it was okay."

"You two friends? Right? Like back from high school days?"

"No, not really."

"Oh?" Rose looked at her as if she expected her to continue.

She sighed. "Yes, we knew each other in high school. All four of us. And Scott and I used to date. We dated seriously. Like really seriously. But then my first year of college—I went away to Wharton, and he stayed back in Colorado—I came home for Christmas." She looked out at the water, watching the sun skip across the tops of the waves. "I was so looking forward to seeing him again. Spending time with him. I'd missed him so much. And he said he needed to talk to me as soon as I got home. We went out by the lake and he…" She swallowed as the memory lunged back, choking her as if it had just been yesterday. She took a steadying gulp of air. "He broke up with me. The last thing I expected. I… I was kind of thinking he was going to ask me to marry him."

"That must have been very painful." Sympathy hovered in Rose's eyes.

"I was heartbroken."

"Why did he break up with you?"

"He said we'd just had a high school thing. We'd grown out of it. That my life was heading in a different direction than his."

"And was it?"

She frowned. "Kind of. I mean, I was away getting my undergrad degree and planned to go on and get my MBA. He was back in Sweet River Falls and never planned on leaving. His mom was there, and she'd done so much for him. Raising him and sacrificing after his dad left. I understood that all along."

"And could you have used your degree in Sweet River Falls?"

"Not at a job like I have now, no. I work at a tech firm. There isn't much of that in Sweet River Falls."

"Did he say he didn't love you anymore?"

"No, not exactly." She thought back, replaying the scene in her mind. "No. He didn't say he didn't love me. Just that it wasn't working out. And I was so crushed that I didn't stop to ask many questions."

"So why don't you ask him now? Ask him

exactly why he broke up with you. Was it someone else? Or maybe he thought he was doing the right thing for you."

"I think he just wasn't interested in me anymore." Her brow creased. Right? He just lost interest.

"Maybe you should ask him." Rose's eyes glimmered with the wisdom of her years. "It's always better to talk things out. Get to the real reason decisions are made."

"I don't know. It was so long ago. I'm not sure it would make any difference."

Rose shrugged. "Maybe. Maybe not. But it could give you some closure. I can still see the pain in your eyes when you told me about it."

"It's in the past. I don't see how dragging up questions about it will help. He did say he was sorry. Repeatedly this week. But sorry doesn't heal old wounds. Doesn't make it any less painful." And it didn't change the fact that she always found a reason to break up with any man when they started getting serious. She had to protect her heart. And really, talking to Scott? How would that protect her heart? It would only bring up more pain. Pain she didn't want to deal with. Especially this week when it should all be about Christie and Tony.

"At least think about it. It seems like you two seeing each other this week might just be fate's way of nudging you to deal with the past."

"I'll think about it." She stood and brushed the sand from her shorts. "I should go. Christie is probably up by now."

"It was nice talking to you. I'm here every morning if you need someone to listen."

"Thanks, Rose." She turned and slowly walked back to the cottage. Was Rose right? Would it help to really talk it out with Scott? Had he been interested in someone else? Had he just lost interest in her? And why hadn't she seen it coming? Maybe it would help to make peace with the past.

Or maybe not. Maybe it would just bring her more pain. Scrape on the still raw gash on her heart.

Now wasn't the time to make that decision. Christie's wedding was in a couple days, and she needed to concentrate on that. And she needed that first cup of coffee. Who made decisions without first having coffee?

Christie sat on a chair by the window, sipping on coffee. "I made a pot." She nodded toward the counter.

Jill walked over, grabbed a cup of the coveted liquid, and sat on the chair next to Christie. She took a sip and sighed. "Ah, that's what I needed."

"Did you go for a walk on the beach?"

"I did. Went to see the sunrise. It was very pretty. Ran into Rose."

"I'm so grateful she can help us with the flowers."

"Me, too. We'll pick them up tomorrow morning after we get your dress from Ruby."

"It's all really coming together, isn't it?" Christie let out a sigh. "I'm so happy with how it's all turning out. I don't know how you made it all come together, but I should never have doubted you. Once you make up your mind and get your lists going, you're unstoppable."

She laughed. "I'm not sure about that, but I really wanted this to work out. Didn't want you to have to cancel or have a wedding that you couldn't look back on and know you had just what you wanted."

"Since it's all planned out now and we're just kind of waiting for tomorrow, Dad and

Tony decided to play golf. Someplace near Sarasota. And Mom and I are going to go shopping in Sarasota, then meet up with them for dinner before heading back. Do you want to come with us?"

"I think I'll just stay here. There are a few more things to check on."

Christie laughed. "I've seen your list. It's checked and double-checked. Why don't you take a day to relax?"

"You guys go ahead." She took another sip of the much-needed coffee. "But I promise, I'll relax some. Really. Maybe I'll even take a book to the beach and read for a while."

Christie looked doubtful. "Promise?"

"I promise." She was making a lot of promises these days...

"Okay. I don't think we'll be late. We have an early dinner reservation, then we'll head back to Moonbeam."

"No hurry on my account. Just go and have a wonderful time."

Christie got up and set her cup in the sink. "I mean it about you taking the day off. Relaxing." She headed back toward her bedroom.

Sure, she'd relax. Right after she went over

her checklist again. She couldn't believe things had fallen into place like this. And she grudgingly admitted Christie was right. Everything was set into place. They just needed to do the flowers tomorrow.

Oh, and she *still* had to write that speech for the reception. She'd sit outside on the porch and write in longhand after Christie left. She could always think better when she wrote things out by hand instead of typing them on her computer.

Then all that was left was the rehearsal. Then the wedding on Sunday. Then she could put all this behind her and go back to her regular, comfortable life.

CHAPTER 17

By late morning, Jill was sitting out on the porch with a glass of iced tea, some Blue Heron Cottages stationery, and her favorite pen with purple ink. She indulged herself with fountain pens, and this one was currently her favorite. Lovely smooth nib. Perfect weight. She conveniently put the thought far from her mind that her whole addiction to fountain pens started in high school when Scott had given her one. And purple ink. He knew she loved purple. She immediately fell in love with the smooth ink flowing across the page. She even learned how to do calligraphy with a stub nib. A simple pleasure that brought her so much joy.

After he broke up with her, she'd almost

thrown away that fountain pen, but she just couldn't. She loved it too much. So she went out and bought a new one to replace it, and the one he gave her was long buried somewhere in some box. Long forgotten. Almost.

Why had all these memories come crashing back now? She grudgingly admitted that the fountain pen from Scott was one of the good memories. The good memories were usually overwhelmed by the memory of the day he broke up with her, though. Wouldn't you think by now she'd be over it? Moved on? She shoved the thoughts aside and started on the task at hand.

She slowly made some notes. Scratched some out in long, smooth strokes. Made some more notes. Soon the pages filled with purple ink and the speech started to take shape.

She set the pen down and took in a deep breath of the salty air. It was so peaceful, just sitting here, the ceiling fan stirring the thick air, the sun splashing light on the gardenia and hibiscus plants scattered around the courtyard. The bright orange and yellow flowers on the hibiscus plants dotted the courtyard with splashes of color.

Scott came out on his porch, waved, and trotted over. "Hey, what's up?" he asked as he climbed the stairs and lounged against the railing.

For once, his very presence didn't irritate her. Hmm, that was different. "I'm just working on my speech for the wedding."

"Ah, that. Haven't started mine."

"Really?" She raised an eyebrow.

"Nah, but I'll think of something."

"You can't just throw something together at the last minute."

He laughed. "I know both of them better than anyone. I'm sure I'll think of something."

How could he do that? Just wing it? She glanced down at her carefully plotted-out speech. And it still needed a lot more work.

"How about we head to the beach? Take some time to relax?"

She eyed him suspiciously. "Christie told you to make sure I took some time off from wedding planning, didn't she?"

He shrugged with an impish smile. "I can neither confirm nor deny that."

"I really should work on my speech."

"And let me disappoint the bride? When she

specifically asked me to do this? Get you to take some time to relax? I don't think that's a good plan."

She sighed and stood up. "Okay, okay. Let's go to the beach."

"Aren't you going to put on your swimsuit?"

"No, these shorts are fine."

"You're going in the water in your shorts?" His eyebrows popped up, questioning her choice.

"I'm not going in the water."

"Hey, I meant go to the beach and go *swimming*. It's ridiculously hot and sticky today."

"I don't do oceans. Or the gulf, or whatever. There are so many creatures in the oceans. Sharks. Stingrays. Jellyfish."

"Oh, come on. Those are over-exaggerated threats. You'll be fine."

She shook her head. Vigorously. "Nope."

"Dare you." His eyes sparkled with challenge.

"How mature." She glared at him.

"Come on. Don't you ever regret not going all the way up to the top of Castlewood Peak with me? Won't you regret never swimming in the sea?"

She wasn't about to admit she *did* regret not just taking his hand and creeping along that ledge and making it to the mountaintop. But surely she wouldn't regret missing a swim in the gulf. Would she?

She chewed her bottom lip.

"Will you at least try it? I swear if you don't like it, we'll come right out of the water."

"Okay, but just for a minute or two. Just to say I did it." And she didn't plan to actually swim. She'd just go in about waist deep to say she'd been in the sea. She still didn't think it was a very good idea. "I'll meet you back out here in fifteen minutes."

He flashed her a self-congratulatory grin. "Perfect. Back in a jiff."

She went inside and headed back to slip on her swimsuit. What in the world had made her say yes? Was she crazy? She put on her suit, then some sunscreen. Found her coverup and a hat. Dug through the closet for her flip-flops. Grabbed a tote bag and loaded it with a couple bottles of water. More sunscreen. A towel. Lip balm. A book. An extra towel—one for sitting on the beach and one for drying off.

Then she couldn't think of any more ways

to procrastinate. She knew she was probably keeping Scott waiting…

"Come on, Jillybean. Daylight is burning," Scott called through the door.

In a fit of resolve, she squared her shoulders and headed outside. She stopped dead in her tracks and stared at Scott, her mouth gaping open.

He stood there in his swim shorts and no shirt, a towel thrown casually over his shoulder. He looked like some kind of Greek god standing there with the sunlight spilling over his tanned chest and shoulders. How did he get a tan like that in Colorado? Did he hike without his shirt on?

He gave her that lazy grin of his. "Like what you see?"

She hastily shoved her sunglasses on. "What? The sun was in my eyes." She stepped off the porch, passed him, and headed for the beach, leaving him to follow.

She found a place in the shade near some trees at the edge of the beach and plopped her tote on the sand.

"Ah, not the shade. Don't you want to get some sun?" He walked up to her and eyed her things sitting in the shade.

"It's hot. And too much sun isn't good for you." And this was further from the water. Maybe they could just sit here in the shade. Stay out of the looming gulf. She took out the towel she'd designated for sitting on and spread it in the sand.

Scott dumped his one towel in a pile on the sand, kicked off his sandals, and laughed. "Looks like you packed half your cottage to come out here to the beach."

"I like to be prepared." She sniffed and turned her back on him, carefully brushing the sand off her tote before placing it on the towel.

"You ready to swim?" He looked at her as if he didn't believe she'd go.

"Of course," she lied as she slipped her coverup over her head and folded it before placing it on the towel.

It was impossible to miss the admiring look he gave her. Her swimsuit was a modest one-piece, much different from the bikinis she'd worn back when they were in high school. But the look in his eyes made her heart flutter. She ignored it and kicked off her flip-flops. She placed the hat on top of the folded coverup and set her sunglasses beside them. She couldn't think of any other way to stall the inevitable. "I'm ready." But she wasn't. Not really.

They headed to the water's edge, her steps slowing the closer they got to the water. She eyed the waves rolling into shore. The breeze had kicked up, and the waves crested in frothy white foam as they spilled over and raced to the shore.

He plunged into the water about waist deep. She stepped in ankle deep and stopped. Then took one more step, and she was almost knee-deep. See, this was fine. She was in the water. She was fine.

Scott dove into the waves, coming up laughing and shaking the water from his hair. "Ah, the water temp is fabulous. Come on in."

She took another tiny step, eyeing the water, searching for jellyfish or other threatening creatures. Or what if she stepped on one of those spiky things? Sea urchins. Weren't they poisonous?

The water was crystal clear here, and she could see the bottom. Was that just a shell down there? Or something… worse? Her heart galloped in her chest when an unexpected wave surged in and splashed her to her waist. She stepped back quickly.

Scott trudged through the water and stood beside her. He reached out his hand. "Come on. I'll walk out with you. It will be okay. I promise."

She stared at his hand, and then in disbelief as her traitorous hand reached out to grasp his. He sent her an encouraging look. "It will be fine."

They took a few slow steps, and the water crept up her legs, up to her waist. "This is far enough."

"Come on, a little bit further. We can jump the waves, ride them in. It's fun."

"Doesn't sound like fun."

"I know you're an excellent swimmer. Have you really never been swimming in the ocean?"

"Never."

"No time like the present." He tugged her hand, urging her to take another step.

She stared in horror as a large wave rolled toward them. "Oh, no."

"Just jump, Jillybean. Just jump."

Scott leapt up, taking her with him, and she rode over the top of the wave, then sank back down to stand on the seafloor.

"See, that wasn't bad, was it?"

No, not bad. Kind of fun, actually. Though she still eyed the water, looking for dangers.

"Here comes another one," he said as he started to jump.

Her hand slipped out of his, and she panicked.

"Jump," he called out.

She pushed off the seafloor and just made it with her head above the wave. Scott swam back to her. "Come on, let's swim down the beach a bit. Get some exercise."

The water did look inviting. It had to be better to swim than stand here and let the waves pummel her. She launched herself into the water and started to swim with a measured crawl stroke she'd learned to perfect swimming in the chilly lake in Sweet River. This wasn't much different. Kind of. She still kept an eye out for sharks.

The water was warm and buoyant and—she had to admit, but only to herself—kind of nice. Scott came up beside her and they swam along a few minutes before turning and heading back up the shoreline.

When they got back even with where their things were on the beach, Scott stopped and stood again in the water. She peered down, not seeing anything dangerous looking that she might step on, and stopped beside him.

"That wasn't so bad, was it?"

"It was... okay."

"Oh, come on. It was better than okay. Aren't you glad you did it?"

She was glad. Glad she'd overcome her fear. Took a risk. With a grin that could match the impish ones he was always throwing her way, she swept her hand in an arc and splashed a wave of water over him.

"Hey." He sputtered and laughed and soon a water fight ensued. He splashed her. She splashed him. Before she knew it, she'd climbed on his back, trying to push him under. They played like young kids, not fifty-year-old adults. And it might have been the most fun she'd had in decades.

Finally, tired, they headed to shore and back up to their belongings. She shook the saltwater out of her hair and carefully dried off with the drying towel, then sank onto the sitting towel.

Scott stood before her, still drying off his tanned body, the sunshine spotlighting him like a stage light. Not that she noticed.

He dropped his towel on the sand and sat beside her. "That was great."

"It was fun," she grudgingly admitted.

"Now, aren't you glad I suggested it?"

"Yes." That was all she was giving him.

"So I was right, and you were… how do they say it? Wrong?" he teased.

"I already said I had fun."

His expression grew sober. "I wish I could have talked you into walking that ledge all those years ago. I wish I could have taken you all the way to the top of Castlewood Peak."

She looked at him for a long moment. "I do, too," she said softly.

Now that was unexpected. Scott never thought he'd hear Jill say she regretted anything. She was definite with her choices. Stood by them.

Of course, he never expected her to take him up on his challenge to go swim in the ocean. She'd been tentative at first, but then they swam side by side, just like they used to at Lone Elk Lake back in Sweet River. Though, the water today was warmer than the water ever got back home.

He looked over at her, her cheeks slightly reddened from the salt and the sun. Her hair hung down around her shoulders in wet clusters. She looked so beautiful it almost took his breath away.

He cleared his throat. "Maybe someday we can try that hike again."

Sadness clouded her eyes. "I don't get back to Sweet River very often."

"Maybe you should come visit more."

"You sound like Christie."

It would be nice if Jill came back to visit. Maybe they could find their way back to being friends. Maybe the four of them could go out if Jill visited. Maybe. So many maybes.

They sat on the beach talking and even went back for another swim. He couldn't remember when he'd had such a good time. It was almost like the old Jill was here. Laughing. Teasing. They splashed and played in the waves like little kids instead of full-grown adults. And he enjoyed every single moment.

They headed back to their spot on the beach when the sun ducked behind a looming cloud.

"Looks like it might storm." Jill peered out in the direction of the gathering clouds.

"It does. It's Florida though. Storms pop up all the time in the late afternoon, then clear up."

"We should probably head back to our cottages."

He didn't want to leave. Leave the magic of their time on the beach. But she was right. It did look like the sky wanted to dump rain. A sudden gust blew their towels as if to make its point.

They picked up their things and headed back to the cottages as the breeze picked up in earnest. They got to her cottage right as a few large drops of rain plopped down around them. He still didn't want to let her go in.

"So, do you want to go get something to eat for dinner?" He eyed her, not sure if she'd turn him down and break the fragile bridge they'd built between them.

"I'm starving after all that swimming." She nodded vigorously.

He grinned, thrilled she'd said yes. "And the horseplay. Can't forget that."

"I do believe I dunked you more than you dunked me."

"I let you win."

She laughed. "Liar."

Okay, maybe this really was going to work. Maybe they could become friends.

"I'll go shower and change. Be back in about a half an hour?"

"Give me forty-five minutes."

"Sure. Forty-five then." He dashed out into the rain and over to his cottage. Glancing back, he saw she was still standing on her porch, watching him. He smiled and waved before slipping inside.

Dinner with Jill. Not exactly a date. But not exactly not one either.

CHAPTER 18

Forty-five minutes later exactly, Jill answered the knock at her door. As Scott stood there, the heavens opened and rain poured down in solid sheets of raindrops.

He laughed. "Looks like I made it over here just in time."

A loud clap of thunder shook the cottage. Winds whipped through the courtyard, making the palm branches dance. She tugged his hand and pulled him inside. "Should we wait a bit for the storm to subside before we leave?"

"That's probably a good idea."

She closed the door against the winds and turned to him. "I have some tea in the fridge. Want some?"

"Sure, sounds good."

She poured two glasses and turned on the table lamp against the darkness creeping across the room as the storm intensified. He settled on the couch beside her, barely twelve inches away. An uncomfortable silence loomed between them. The only sound was the tinkling of the ice against the glasses and the rain pelting the roof. He was so close. So familiar. And yet... so different.

He finally set his glass on the table and turned to look directly at her. "So, we're back to awkward silences again? We were doing so well on the beach. Thought maybe we could be friends again."

"We're... friends." She knew her words sounded tentative.

"Are we?" He eyed her.

"We're getting there," she said softly.

A loud smash of thunder startled her, and she jumped, landing closer to Scott on the couch.

"That was a loud one," he said.

She scooted back away from him. "Yes, sorry. It just surprised me."

Another loud boom and a long flash of lightning. Then another rumble. The wind rattled the cottage. Rain hammered the roof. Unease settled over her.

"Quite the storm out there." Scott eyed her closely.

Her glance darted to the window and caught another flash of lightning.

"You okay? You never were a fan of storms."

"Sure. I'm fine." It sounded like a lie to her own ears, and she was certain he didn't believe her either. She jumped at the next clap of thunder as the wind picked up to a roar. Suddenly they were plunged into darkness and her heart took off in a riotous beat.

"Looks like we lost electricity." Scott's voice sounded in the darkness as he slid next to her and put an arm around her shoulder.

She trembled slightly—either from the storm or being so close to him—but welcomed the safety and security of his arm.

"Guess we'll just wait it out. I'm sure it will die down soon." His soothing words filtered through the darkness.

It couldn't be soon enough for her. It sounded like the wind was the big bad wolf, and he was going to accomplish his goal of blowing the cottage down. Something hit the side of the house and she screamed.

"It'll be okay." He pulled her closer to him and stroked her hair.

She sat beside him, letting him comfort her as the storm raged outside. Finally, after what seemed like an eternity but probably was more like half an hour, the winds began to ebb and the thunder moved off into the distance. Still, she didn't move away from him.

"See, I knew it would end soon," he whispered against her forehead, his warm breath lingering on her cheek.

Her heart skittered, and her pulse raced, and this time it was not from the storm. He was so close. Arms wrapped around her like it was just the two of them, alone in the world.

Her phone lit up the darkness, and she grabbed it, seeing it was from Christie. "Hey." She managed to force out one word, trying to concentrate, ignoring how Scott loosened his hold on her and she suddenly felt adrift.

"Oh, Jill. We've been in an accident. We're okay, but it was so scary."

"Slow down. Tell me what happened." She switched the phone to speaker, panic racing through her.

"We were driving and a terrible storm came through. A car came out of nowhere and hit us."

"Oh, no. Is everyone alright?"

"Yes. But we're at the hospital now. Mom got cut by the glass and is getting a few stitches. And Tony…" Christie's voice cracked. "Tony hurt his ankle. I'm afraid he'll be on crutches for the wedding."

"That's okay. I'm sure he'll rock those crutches. I'm just so glad it wasn't worse."

"Dad's car is totaled, and everyone is a bit shaken up. It's still storming, so Dad got us rooms here in town for the night. No one felt like venturing out in the storm again. We've rented a car for tomorrow and we'll be back in Moonbeam first thing in the morning. I know there is so much to do."

"Don't worry about that. We'll get it all done. I'm so glad everyone is okay with only minor injuries." Relief swept through her that none of them were seriously hurt.

"Me, too. Are you going to be okay there by yourself?"

"Sure, I'll be fine." She didn't mention Scott was right here with her. Dangerously close.

"Did Moonbeam get hit by this same storm?"

"A little bit." No use worrying her about the storm and how the electricity was out. Surely it would be back on by tomorrow morning. Hopefully it would be back on sooner than that. Like any minute.

"Okay, here's Mom coming out to the waiting room. We're going to head to the hotel. I'll see you in the morning."

"See you then." She clicked off the phone. The sky began to brighten outside, and early evening light filtered in through the windows.

"That's too bad about the accident." Scott was no longer holding her but still didn't move away. She didn't know how she felt about that.

A knock at the door saved her from overanalyzing her feelings. She jumped up to answer it. Violet stood on the other side, her arms laden. "Just coming to check on you and make sure you're okay. Oh hi, Scott."

Scott walked up behind her. "We're fine."

"I brought you a battery-powered lantern and here are some candles." Violet handed them to her. "We're never sure how long the electricity will be out from these storms. Wow, that one just popped up out of nowhere, didn't it?"

"It was quite the storm." She didn't elaborate on her not-so-stoic reaction to it.

"Be careful with the candles."

"We will," Scott assured her.

"I need to go check on the other cottages. Call the office if you need anything."

"Oh, Christie, Tony, and her parents are staying in Sarasota for the night, so no need to check on them. A bit of an accident, but everyone is okay. They just didn't want to brave the weather again."

"That's probably smart. I'll go check on Rose. Glad you two are okay. Oh, and here. I brought this basket of food. Heard the electricity is out all through town, so there won't be any restaurants open. Luckily I had a fresh loaf of bread from Evelyn and some sandwich makings. There are sandwiches, fruit, and cookies in there. Hope that can tide you over tonight."

"That was really nice of you." Jill took the basket.

"If you need anything, just ask. Sorry about the electricity."

"That's okay. We'll be fine." Scott closed the

door as Violet hurried away on her mission to check on the guests.

Scott flipped on the lantern and held it high, tossing its beam around the room. "How about we light some candles? Looks like the last of the daylight is fading quickly."

She placed some candles on a few plates and scattered them around, giving the room a warm, soft glow. Scott pulled the food out of the basket and set it out on plates.

"I think I'll turn off the lantern and save the batteries if the candlelight is okay with you."

She nodded, and the room came alive with the soft glow of the candles. And here she was, more than thirty years later, having a candlelight dinner with Scott. Who would have ever thought that would happen?

Scott sat across from Jill at the small cafe table in the cottage. The candlelight wrapped them in an intimate blanket. She concentrated on her sandwich as if it were the most interesting thing in the world. That awkward silence he'd grown to hate settled over them again.

"So, this isn't so bad, is it?"

"No, the sandwiches are great. This sourdough bread Evelyn made is wonderful."

"I was talking more about being stuck here for dinner…"

She glanced up quickly. "No, it's not so bad. Especially since the storm seems to have subsided."

Right then, a rumble of thunder sounded in the distance. "Or maybe we'll get another one come through."

"I hope not."

"You know, I could stay here at the cottage tonight. Especially with the electricity being off. And in case another big storm comes."

"Oh, I'll be okay." She didn't sound convincing.

"I'm sure you will be, but it would make me feel better if I stayed here. I think it would be a good idea."

"Maybe."

Well, that wasn't a definite no. And he'd worry about her all night if he went back to his cottage. She wasn't good in any storm unless things had really changed in the last thirty years. And judging by how jumpy she'd been earlier, he didn't think she'd changed her opinion of storms.

Jill got up from the table. "I have a bottle of red wine. Would you like a glass?"

He paused. "Yes, okay. A small glass."

She puttered around pouring the wine, maybe avoiding his question or maybe just to cut through the nervous energy that had them in its grip.

She finally sat down and handed him a glass, careful to make sure their fingers didn't touch.

"So, Tony is going to get married on crutches." He couldn't think of anything else to talk about.

"Sounds that way."

"Glad no one was really hurt."

"Uh-huh." She nodded.

This wasn't working out. Just reiterating what they both knew. He tried again. "So, do you still read all the time?"

She looked up quickly, surprise in her eyes. "You remember that?"

"Of course. I remember everything, Jillybean. That you like your coffee black. You were so determined to learn to like coffee and that it would have to be black. Not disguised with cream and sugar. Took you over a month, and then suddenly you were like coffee's most devoted fan."

"I still am." Her lips curved in a gentle smile.

There, that was better. "And I remember your favorite color is purple."

"Oh, no." She leapt up from the table and rushed to the door, throwing it open. "Oh, no."

He got up and hurried over to the door. "What's wrong? What did I say?"

"My speech. I left it out here on the table with my pen. The papers are gone and so is my favorite fountain pen."

She still wrote with fountain pens. Ever since that first one he'd given her. That made him unreasonably happy. "I guess you'll just have to wing the speech."

She whirled around. "Just because you're not going to be prepared doesn't mean I'm not."

"Okay, okay." He put his hands up and backed away. "You'll just have to rewrite it then."

"If I can remember what I decided on." Frustration punctuated each word.

"I'm sure it all will come back to you." He tried to ease her discouragement. "Come on, let's finish our meal."

She sighed, crossed over to the table, and sank onto her chair. He sat down across from her, afraid to say anything wrong. After the awkward silence began to bug him again, he asked, "And you know what else I remember?"

She raised her eyebrows.

"The way you get bright pink spots on your cheeks when you're exasperated with me."

"I do not…" She frowned. "Do I?"

"Yep. And you like to watch Christmas movies any time of the year. Christmas lights have to have all the colors, not just white. Your favorite pie is peach. You don't like nuts in your cookies. And you love the scent of pine trees."

Her mouth dropped open, and she stared at Scott. How did he remember all that? And he was wrong. She liked nuts in her cookies now, but that had only happened in the last few years and she had no idea what had changed her mind.

"And how about you, Jillybean? Do you remember much about me?" He looked across at her, waiting.

"Not much. It was so long ago." That was such a lie. His favorite color was blue. He preferred apple pie. If he ever spent much money on himself, it was for good hiking boots. He got excited when they'd see a bald eagle fly overhead. And he loved winter. The snow, the cold, the crisp air.

"Nothing?" He eyed her.

"Some."

"My favorite color?"

"Blue," she said automatically before she could catch herself.

"Favorite food."

"Pizza."

He grinned. "So you do remember some things."

"Of course I do." She sighed. "You loved the Star Wars movies. I bet you've seen every one of them."

"I have. Multiple times."

"You like to sit out and stare up at the stars and you know most of the constellations. You can make a fire in like thirty seconds flat. I'll never understand how you do that. You wear shorts when it's way too cold for it. You don't like hoodies."

"I don't. The hoods bug me."

He gave her one of *those* grins. The ones that hovered on his lips and used to make her heart skitter—and evidently still did.

"What else do you remember?" His eyebrows rose.

"I remember... a lot."

"Do you ever think of the good times we had? Swimming in the lake? Picnics? Hanging out with Christie and Tony?"

"Sometimes."

Rose's voice popped into her head. *Ask him. Ask him why he broke up with you.*

She took a deep breath, not sure she was ready for his answers. "Can I ask you something?"

"Of course. Anything."

"Why did you break up with me? I mean the real reason."

CHAPTER 19

J ill pinned him with a look so intense it was impossible for him to look away. So he met her gaze and considered his options.

"I… Ah… are you sure you want to know? It's complicated." He did not want to have this conversation. He'd do anything to keep from hurting her.

"I don't care if it's complicated. I want to know the truth. Not the nonsense that we'd grown apart. Were you seeing someone else?"

"What? No. That wasn't it," he quickly assured her. Did she really think he'd cheat on her? But then, he hadn't given her much of an explanation all those years ago. He couldn't.

"Then what was it?" She leaned back in her chair and crossed her arms.

"We just grew up. Grew apart." She knew there was more than that. He could see it in her eyes.

"No, I want the *whole* truth."

He debated, still unsure. It was so long ago. Best left in the past.

She sat there staring at him, a determined look on her face. He knew she wasn't going to let it drop, and he wasn't willing to lie to her. Not now.

He sighed. "Okay. I'll tell you, but you're not going to like it."

"I don't care if I won't like it. I want the truth. I *deserve* the truth."

"Yes, you probably do." He took a deep breath. "So… here goes. Your father came and talked to me."

"Dad? What did he talk to you about?"

"How you were off to great things. A good degree from an elite school. You had all these opportunities ahead of you. How I should just let you go. I'd only be holding you back. You didn't have a future in Sweet River, and I was never going to leave. Not after all my mom had done for me. I'd never leave her alone."

She sat there in stunned silence, then finally said, "My dad always pushed me—hard—to apply to good schools, get good grades, be the best. I knew he wasn't thrilled you and I were dating. But this? I never would have thought he was capable of this. He knew how much I cared about you. And he was ever so supportive when I was so upset about the breakup. Of course he was. He'd caused it all and gotten his way, yet again."

"I'm sorry, Jill. Sorry how it all played out."

A frown wrinkled her forehead. "But why did you listen to him?"

"Because... he was right. You did have so many opportunities ahead of you. Look at all you have. A great job. Up for a promotion. Christie says you have this really fancy condo. You'd have none of that if you were still tied down to me."

"Tied down? I wasn't *tied down*. I... I loved you."

"And I loved you. Enough to let you go and have the best life possible."

"Dad shouldn't have interfered. You and I could have worked things out. Found a way for both of us to have what we needed. We could have figured that all out together." Her eyes burned with pain mixed with anger.

He let out a long sigh. "Maybe. But I was

young then. And your father was rather… forceful."

Her eyes narrowed. "What do you mean by that?"

He paused, wondering if it was really right to tell her this. But it was the truth. And part of the reason he'd done what her father asked. "I'm sorry. I never wanted you to hear all this."

"Just tell me. All of it."

"Mom had just lost her job. The shop she was working at closed. Your father…" He paused, hating what he was getting ready to explain.

"Tell me."

"He implied he'd talk to Old Man Dobbs about making sure Mom had a hard time finding a new job. I couldn't risk that."

"He what?" Her eyes flashed with anger. "That's so unfair. So wrong." Then suddenly the anger deflated and her shoulders sank. "I'm so, so sorry. He never should have done that."

"It's not your fault. It's just how everything worked out."

She leaned forward and took his hands in hers. Electricity that rivaled the lightning in the storm that had just ended jolted through him.

"And all this time I've been so mad at you.

Always wondering why you broke up with me. What I'd done. I've let that anger consume me for years, but it appears I've been angry with the wrong person." She shook her head, "And I can't even yell at him now unless it's by going out to his grave and giving him a piece of my mind. Which I probably will do if I ever make it back to Sweet River."

"I'm sorry. I don't want to tarnish your memories of him." But carrying this secret all these years had been a burden. And he always questioned whether he'd made the right choice.

"No, I'm glad you told me. And I guess I shouldn't be surprised. Dad always wanted things to go his way. He was pretty determined in his choices."

And she was her father's daughter, but he thought it best not to say so. Just as determined in her choices, but hopefully not choices that affected people's lives so drastically it caused them to veer off the track they were on.

She jumped up, paced back and forth, then walked over to the window, staring outside. He got up and went to stand beside her, giving her time to process all he'd told her. She finally turned and looked up at him, a sadness emanating from her eyes that squeezed his heart. "I don't even know where to go with this. What to think. I'm just so sorry. So sad. So frustrated."

"I know, Jillybean. From my perspective of the years now, I wish I would have just talked it out with you. Told you then what your dad said."

"Except for his threat against your mom. And Dobbs likes nothing better than causing trouble. I understand why you did it. It was probably the right choice at the time." She snaked her arms around his waist and he pulled her close, stroking her silky hair.

They stood there, watching the sky darken and a few stars pop out as if defying any mention of the earlier storm.

She turned in his arms, facing him. "Scotty, you know what?"

Scotty. She'd called him Scotty. Just like all those years ago. "Hmm?"

"I would like you to stay here at the cottage tonight. You know, just in case another storm comes through."

He grinned. "So... I was right, and you were—"

She held up a hand, cutting him off, and shook her head. "Don't say it."

Jill finally pulled back from Scott's embrace. "We should probably finish our dinner."

"Probably." But he didn't let her go.

"Aren't you hungry?"

"Not particularly."

She laughed. "Liar. You're always hungry."

"Okay, maybe a little bit."

She slipped out of his arms and sat down at the table. He followed and sat across from her. They sat and talked about this and that. But in her mind, all she could think about was her father. What he had done. How it had changed her whole life. And she'd never known. Always blamed Scott. Harbored such a burning anger toward him. It had consumed her, and her therapist told her was unhealthy and she should deal with it. But she never had. Somehow, that anger had become her armor. Her protection from ever getting hurt again.

"Hey, you still with me?" Scott asked.

"Oh, I'm sorry. I'm a bit lost in thought."

"It was a lot to take in all at once. I'm still not sure I should have told you. He was your father, after all. I hate to muddy up your memories of him."

189

"It was the right thing to do to tell me. Really it was." She got up from the table. "I'm going to get more wine. Want some?"

"Um, nah, I'm good."

She hated to have a second if he wasn't going to join her, but she wanted one. She wavered, her hand by the bottle.

"Go ahead." He laughed. "I've just barely started my glass."

She poured herself a refill and sat down. "So, let's talk about something other than my father. Tell me all about your company."

"It's called Wild Eagle Expeditions. I have three full-time employees and a handful of part-time guides I call on when needed. We offer all sorts of guided trips depending on the season. Hiking, skiing, backpacking, snowshoeing. I'm teaming up with a white-water rafting company to offer that soon, too. Oh, and I found a guy that will teach rappelling next summer."

His eyes lit up when he talked about his company. The name of the company didn't surprise her. He did love watching the eagles soar.

"And how about your job?" He leaned back in his chair.

"I work for a tech company. A sales

manager. I talk to companies and try to sell our services to them."

"Bet you're their number one salesperson."

She blushed. "I am."

He grinned.

"I'm up for a promotion to upper management. Not sure how I feel about that. I won't see much of the sales side anymore. It will be more managing the managers."

"Ah, corporate life. Managers of managers. Do you like what you do?"

"I... do. Mostly. I'm getting tired of the travel, but I'll still have lots of it if I get the promotion because I'll have to go visit with all our regional managers."

"What would you rather do?"

She paused, wondering if she could share her dream. "I have a couple of ideas for some apps that I'd like to try and launch. A social media app full of interest groups where people could gather and share information. Simple to use. No politics, though. Hopefully, a safe space for everyone. And another app that would be an easy way for people to coordinate their remodeling projects. And one that writers could use to track everything from projects to word count to income and expenses, all in one place."

"That's a lot of ideas."

"Oh, I have more." She laughed. "I've played around with programming them, but I'd have to hire someone who's better than me to actually program them and get all the details right. I just have a rough prototype. But I don't have time to really get into them with all the hours I put into my job."

"They sound like interesting projects."

"Yes, well, if I ever have time, maybe I'll get somewhere with one of them."

"Why don't you make time?"

"I…" Why didn't she make time? Why was she always making excuses? "I don't know. Maybe I should."

He grinned at her. "You could put it on one of your lists. Schedule it in. Then you could check it off. You love that."

"Ha, ha. Very funny." But it wasn't a bad suggestion. If she listed it off on her weekly to-do list for, say, six to eight hours a week, she'd maybe get somewhere with one of the ideas. Maybe she would even quit going into the office on Sundays…

"Follow your dreams, Jill."

"It's kind of late in life to start all over, isn't it?"

"Nah, it's never too late to chase a dream."

"Maybe." She chewed her bottom lip. The urge to actually sit down and make a list of things she'd need to do to start really working on one of these projects poked at her. But not tonight. The list could wait. Tonight she was sitting here in the candlelight with Scott.

They finished their dinner and moved over to the couch. She leaned against Scott as he put his arm around her shoulder. They talked until the wee hours of the morning, as her mom used to say.

And it felt so right sitting here with him. They'd always been able to talk for hours, with the minutes just flying by, and tonight was no exception. The last words she remembered were him talking about an eagle's nest high up in an evergreen on the trail to Castlewood Peak.

CHAPTER 20

Jill stirred. She shifted slightly, a crick in her neck nagging her awake. As she slowly came around, she realized she was in Scott's arms, snuggled up against him on the couch. Slowly, she started to push upright, but he tightened his arms around her. She gingerly pried his hold on her and slipped out from under his arm.

His eyes popped open, and a sleepy smile crept over his lips. "Well, good morning."

"Morning." She sat up the rest of the way and rubbed her neck.

He levered himself upright and stretched, moving his head from side to side. "Guess we didn't pick the most comfortable place to sleep with two perfectly good beds in the cottage."

195

"Guess not." Not that she would have invited him to her bed. She was barely used to being friends with him again.

He got up, stretched again, and walked over to flip the light switch. "Nothing."

"I hope it comes back on soon. We've got so much to do today for the wedding and we'll need refrigeration for the flowers. Evelyn needs electricity to prepare the food. What are we going to do if it doesn't come back on?"

"We'll figure it out. There's still a lot of time left before we need to worry."

"And most importantly, how am I going to get my coffee this morning?" She painted on a smile, trying to head off her panic.

Just then, a knock sounded, and Scott opened the door. Violet stood there with a thermos in her hand. "Brought you coffee."

She jumped up and had to stop from launching herself at Violet. "You are like my very best friend right now."

Violet laughed. "My brother got an old camp stove working, and we made some. I need my coffee, too. I've got a thermos for you, and one for Rose. I've made another pot, so if you need more, just pop into the office."

"Any news when the electricity might come back on?" Scott asked.

"No, nothing yet. It's the whole town. A main transformer blew plus a lot of downed power lines. They're working on it. I'll let you know if I hear something more."

"Okay, thanks."

Jill looked past Violet and out at the courtyard. "Oh, no. Look at the mess." Downed branches were strewn across the area. A few chairs were blown over. The arbor that had been put up yesterday was blown over and a side broken off.

"Don't worry about that. Rob promised to help work on clearing it up. We'll drag out the downed palm branches. Clean out the debris. Put the arbor back up. Get things all sorted. It will look fine, I promise."

"I can help later today if you need me," Scott offered.

"Might take you up on that." Violet bobbed her head. "Let me get this coffee to Rose."

Violet disappeared as Jill took the thermos over to the counter and poured two steaming cups of coffee. So much better to face the day after a cup of coffee.

They settled back on the couch. She took

one sip, then jumped up and grabbed a tablet of paper.

"Need another list?" he teased.

"Yes. A list of what to do if the electricity stays out."

He reached out and took the pen from her hand. "Drink your coffee first. Maybe the electricity will come back on and you won't have to worry about it."

"Maybe. But I like to be prepared for all contingencies." But drinking the coffee without rushing into list-making sounded like a nice way to spend a few more minutes. After that, for sure, she was starting a list. Just to be prepared. Just in case.

She settled back on the couch, telling herself to relax. But her thoughts ping-ponged back to last night. The revelation about what her father had done. How it had affected her life. And Scott's life. How Scott had been forced to make a hard choice. So many thoughts and feeling warred in her mind.

Suddenly, she put down her coffee cup, reached over, and grabbed Scott's hand. "You know last night you asked if we were friends? If we could become friends?"

He cocked his head and nodded.

"I think we can. I hope we can. But let's promise each other that we'll never keep secrets from each other ever again."

He sat down his cup and looked at her for a long moment. "Ah—"

The door flew open, and Christie rushed into the cottage. "We're back." Tony followed behind her, awkwardly clomping along on his crutches.

She jumped up and hugged Christie. "What a night you had. Are you okay?"

"We are." Christie looked over at Scott and raised an eyebrow. "Well, good morning. You're up and over here early this morning."

Scott jumped up and got a chair for Tony, helping him sit, taking his crutches, and leaning them against the wall. "You know me. Early riser."

Christie leaned close and whispered to her, "Weren't you wearing that outfit yesterday when I left?"

She looked down at her wrinkled clothes. "Ah... yes."

Christie raised one eyebrow and smiled but said nothing else.

Ignoring the heat of a blush that warmed

her cheeks, she pointed to the paper on the table. "I was just making a list for today."

"Of course you were." Christie laughed. "But you already have one all written up for today. With a timeline. I saw it."

"There's been a slight complication."

Christie eyed her warily. "And that is?"

"The electricity is out in the whole town of Moonbeam."

Christie walked over to the light switch and flipped it up and down. "No, it can't be."

"Well, it is. But I'm working on how we're going to deal with this."

"But the flowers and the food and… everything. And the storm brought a bit cooler weather, but it will still be sweltering hot to get ready without air-conditioning. And no electricity for my blow dryer or light to put on my makeup." Christie's eyes grew wide with panic.

"It will be okay. We'll figure it out." Did she sound convincing? Was it just another promise in the long line of promises she'd made this week that she had no idea if she could keep? Because she wasn't certain she could make this work if the electricity didn't come back on.

Christie didn't look convinced.

She put on a careful, encouraging smile. "And we should get ready to head over to Belle Island. Rose will be here in a few minutes. She wants to ride over with us to get the flowers. We'll get your dress and then go to the floral shop."

Tony awkwardly pushed off his chair. "Hand me the crutches, will you, Scott? We should get out of here and let the girls get ready."

"We should. And I offered to help clean up the courtyard."

"Looks like I won't be much help to you there." Tony smiled wryly and turned to Christie. "But don't you worry, babe. I'm going to be practicing my crutch walking. I'll be a champion at it by tomorrow."

Jill eyed him standing unsteadily on his crutches. She hoped he didn't fall flat on his face during the ceremony.

Christie went over and kissed him. "I'm sure you will. But it looks like your crutches will be the least of our worries if the electricity doesn't come back on."

Tony headed to the door and Scott walked over to her and leaned close. "We should still talk."

She nodded. They would. But not until she got this wedding all sorted out.

An hour or so later, Jill, Christie, and Rose got to Ruby's house. "There you are. I heard the electricity was out in all of Moonbeam." Ruby ushered them inside out of the stifling humidity. Jill mentally added a note to her ever-growing list. Find some way to keep Christie cool as she was getting ready.

"I'm sure they'll get it sorted out and the electricity will be back on soon," Jill said with authority. Assuredness. Self-confidence. But in all honesty, she had no idea if it would be back on or not.

"Ruby, this is Rose. Rose, Ruby. Rose is helping us with the flowers." Christie introduced Rose.

"Nice to meet you, Rose. So nice of you to help with the flowers." Ruby turned to Christie. "Go try on the dress. Let's make sure it's perfect." Ruby shooed her down the hallway.

Ruby motioned to a couple of large baskets sitting on the table. "Oh, and Tally—she said you all met her the other day at Magic Cafe—

knew you were coming over today, so she packed up baskets of food for you to take back. Sandwiches, Cookies. Cheese and crackers. She didn't want you to worry about finding food along with all the wedding preparations."

"How did she hear…"

"I was at Magic Cafe last night after the storm blew through. We were luckier than Moonbeam. Didn't lose our electricity. Anyway, I mentioned Christie was coming over for her dress today. Tally dropped by these baskets after she heard the electricity was still out in Moonbeam this morning."

"That was so nice of her."

"We all like to look out for each other around here," Ruby said.

They all turned around when Christie entered the room. "Oh, Christie. You look so lovely." Jill stared at her friend. The dress looked like it had been custom made, stitch by stitch, just for her, not years ago for someone else.

Christie slowly twirled around. "It's just perfect, isn't it?"

"It's lovely, dear," Rose said. "You make a beautiful bride."

Ruby walked all around Christie, eyeing her

carefully. "Yes, I think it's perfect. I wouldn't change a thing."

"I should go slip out of it. We still have so much to do today."

"I have a garment bag hanging on the back of the door. Slip it into that to make sure it stays nice and clean."

Christie changed back into her clothes and they headed out. Christie paused at the door. "Ruby, I can't thank you enough for squeezing me in and altering the dress for me."

"I was glad to help. Can't have a bride with no wedding dress, now can we?" Ruby waved to them from the doorway as they pulled away.

They drove to Flossie's Flower Shop and Rose popped out and headed into the shop. Jill and Christie trailed behind. They found Rose deep in discussion with the owner.

"Is something wrong?" Christie asked.

And who could blame her for thinking something was wrong? They'd been thrown a series of obstacles all week.

Rose turned around. "Nothing. We were just discussing how to keep the flowers fresh if the electricity doesn't come on. We have some ideas. It will be fine. You let me worry about the flowers."

They hauled the flowers in large coolers out to the car and headed back toward Moonbeam. Jill kept her fingers crossed all the way back that the electricity would be back on when they arrived.

Scott helped Rob clean up the courtyard while Tony waved his crutch around, giving directions. "Very helpful, buddy," Scott called out when Tony held out his crutch and pointed out yet another downed palm branch.

The day might not be as hot as yesterday, but it was plenty warm. Sweat ran down his back, and he wiped his face with the bottom of his t-shirt. Violet came out with lemonade. He gratefully took a glass, and they took a break in the shade. By mid-afternoon, the courtyard showed hardly a sign of the storm that blew through.

Scott handed his rake to Rob. "I think we've done it. Christie will be pleased." In truth, he was trying to please Jill.

"Thanks for all your help." Rob headed off toward the shed.

Scott turned to Tony, leaning against a

nearby railing. "I'm going to go grab a cold shower, then I have an errand to run."

"Wedding stuff?"

"Nah, just something I need to pick up."

They walked back to the cottage, Tony swinging through each step on his crutches—and not very steadily.

"You're not going to fall walking Christie back down the aisle after the ceremony, are you?"

"I hope not. She'd never let me live it down." Tony sank onto a chair on the porch and glanced up at the nonmoving ceiling fan. "Wish that thing could stir up a bit of movement in this humid air."

"Yeah, the storm dropped the temps a bit but brought in the humidity. I don't think we came out ahead on the deal."

He collapsed on the chair next to Tony. He really needed that shower, but he wouldn't mind a few moments of rest. He wiped the sweat from his face, wishing he had another glass of that lemonade.

"So, you and Jill." Tony leaned back in his chair, wrestling with his crutches until he gave up and dropped them to lean against a nearby chair.

"There is no Jill and me." He shook his head. "Nothing to see there."

"Really? Because I'd swear you spent the night over there at her cottage. Didn't you?"

"I did... but not like that. She was just jumpy from the storm."

"Yeah, Jill hates storms. Always has."

"And with the electricity out and everything." He shrugged. "I offered to stay."

"Surprised she said yes..." Tony eyed him. "Though it looks like you two are getting along better."

"We are, I think so anyway." He stretched out his legs, the shower still calling for him, but he didn't have the energy to get up and go inside just yet. Between the lack of sleep last night and the hard labor in the courtyard, he was beat. Not that he minded the lack of sleep. He'd enjoyed every minute of sitting in the low light in the cottage talking until all hours with Jill. Catching up with what she'd been doing with her life. Talking about anything and everything, just like it used to be before he'd blown them all up. Then she'd fallen asleep, curled up next to his side. He had no idea how long he'd sat there just staring at her sleeping. Tucking a wayward lock of hair back so he could see her long lashes resting against her flushed cheeks.

Tony shifted in his chair, knocking a crutch to the ground. It clattered on the wooden planks of the porch, and Tony grimaced before turning to him. "Anyway, I'm glad things are better between you two."

"We talked a bit. I… I finally told her the reason I broke up with her."

Tony's eyes flickered with surprise. "You did? About what her dad told you and threatened to do and everything?"

"Yep, everything."

"About time. So she'll probably talk to Christie about it, who will come and tell me, and I'll have to act surprised like I didn't know the whole truth for all these years."

"No, you can tell her you knew. But I appreciate you keeping my secret all this time. I didn't want Jill to be hurt by what her father did. And… well, the man had a bit of truth to what he said. I would have held her back."

Tony shook his head. "No, you wouldn't have. But I told you that thirty years ago."

He sent Tony a wry look. "And I wish I would have listened to you. Things would be so different now."

"They would. But maybe you have another chance now. She's not seeing anyone. You're not seeing anyone."

"We live half a country apart."

"So?"

"I don't know. We're barely back to the just friends stage."

Tony leaned forward in his chair. "If you are going to be friends or even try to be more than friends, there's something you have to do, you know."

He let out a long sigh. "I know."

Tony locked his gaze on him. "You have to tell her about your marriage."

CHAPTER 21

Violet propped the door open to the office, hoping that some semblance of a breeze would filter through. Rob and Scott had done a great job cleaning up the courtyard and had the arbor back in place. Tomorrow they'd set out the tables and chairs, but for now, things were looking good. She hoped things stayed that way. There had been enough complications with Christie's wedding, but things seemed to be turning out okay.

The photographer had agreed to give her some shots from the wedding to put up on the Blue Heron Cottages website. She needed them to help promote the cottages as a wedding venue. She, in turn, would recommend the photographer to people looking at the cottages for a venue.

But the key problem remaining was they really needed the electricity to come back on.

She turned as Christie and Jill came through the doorway, carrying a large cooler between them. "We're back," Jill said as they set the cooler down.

"Good. I set up that table over there for Rose to have lots of room to work."

Rose came in with another smaller cooler and a bag of ribbons and lace.

"I'll get the rest of the stuff." Jill went out and returned with another cooler and a bag.

"I've got some good news." Violet handed each of them a glass of lemonade. "Rob left a bit ago, heading to Sarasota to get a generator. Been meaning to get one and now seemed like a good time. I have two fridges. One in the back room of the office and one in my owner suite. We'll hook the generator up to them. So we'll have two fridges to put the flowers in. And, if the electricity doesn't come back on by tomorrow—but I sure hope it does—if you need to come to my suite to get ready, we'll plug the generator into a window air-conditioner unit and cool the place down."

"Oh, that would be great," Christie said.

"And I found that box of old mason jars Rose wanted to use for vases on the tables. They're in pretty good shape, considering who knows how long they were in the shed. I have them all washed up."

"Thank you. I think they'll work out nicely." Rose started setting out ribbon and lace on the table.

"Oh, and Donna—she owns Parker's General Store—had some solar fairy lights. She dropped them off so they can charge in the sun today, and we'll use them to decorate the arbor. And she had some solar lanterns at her house that she brought over that we can put around for lighting." Violet tried to remember what else she'd taken care of today.

"I can't believe how so many people are chipping in to help us." Christie's eyes glistened with gratitude.

"Evelyn said that if the electricity comes on by morning, she'll still be able to make the food but will have to adjust the menu some," Violet added. "She had a generator at the cafe, but only enough to keep the big fridge going."

"I'm fine with that. I just really would like to have food at the reception." Christie shrugged.

"With all the curves thrown at this wedding, I'll just be glad if we can pull it off."

"We know there will at least be cake. Julie is delivering it tomorrow. Luckily Belle Island has electricity." Jill turned to Christie. "Why don't you go check on Tony? See how's he doing? I'll stay here and work with Rose and Violet and do the flowers."

"I should stay and help."

"No, you go see Tony. Rest some. We've got this," Rose said as she sat down and picked up a handful of daisies.

"If you're sure."

"Go." Jill pushed Christie toward the door.

Violet sat down beside Rose. "So, I know nothing about making bouquets, but just tell me what to do."

"I'm going to go ahead and make up the bridal bouquet. And sort out the flowers for the tables. I'll put them in the vases tomorrow and set them on the tables right before the wedding starts. But I also got some extra ribbon. I thought we could tie matching bows on the chairs along the walkway to the arbor. And tomorrow I'll add some flowers to the arbor along with the fairy lights Violet found."

"Do you want me to make up the bows for the chairs? I tie a mean bow. I like to make presents look fancy and watched a million bow-making videos online until I perfected my skill," Jill offered.

Rose handed her the spools of ribbon. "Perfect, that's all yours."

They all worked and chatted like old friends. And Rose had become a friend to her, Violet realized. She'd miss her when she finally checked out and went home. But for now, Rose made no noise about leaving. She seemed to be enjoying her stay here in Moonbeam.

Rob came back with the generator and got it hooked up. They put the flowers in the two fridges and stuffed some bags of ice he brought into the freezer compartment.

They all tromped back into the office after safely stashing the flowers.

Rob leaned against the reception counter, sipping on some lemonade. "Oh, and I made a few stops on the way back. Picked up burgers and buns. Chips. Cold beer and soda, all iced up in a cooler. I know it's not the nice rehearsal dinner Violet said you were going to have at The Cabot Hotel, but their restaurant is closed down until the electricity comes on. Hope that will be okay with the bride and groom."

"Let me text Christie. I'm sure she'll love the idea. We'd already discussed just canceling the whole idea of a rehearsal dinner unless everyone drove into Sarasota or over to Belle Island. And Christie wasn't very keen on that after their accident in Sarasota yesterday." Jill grabbed her phone and in a few moments, her face broke into a grin. "Christie always overdoes it with the emojis, but she has a high five, a smiley face, a big grin, and then a GIF of a woman doing a happy dance."

Violet laughed. "I guess that's a yes."

"That was so nice of you." Jill gave Rob a hug. "Everyone here in Moonbeam has been so helpful. So giving."

"That's Moonbeam for you. They all chipped in and helped me paint and fix up the place when I got hurt a while ago." Violet smiled, remembering how it seemed like half the town came to help repair porches and paint buildings and help her in any way they could. "So, we'll meet in the courtyard about six?"

"Perfect. We'll see you in a little bit then." Jill turned to Rose. "And you're coming, too, right?"

"Oh, if you want me to."

"Of course we do. You're practically part of the wedding party now, with all the help you've given us." Jill threaded her arm through Rose's and they headed out.

Violet turned to Rob. "And you'll get the grills started and cook?"

Rob rolled his eyes. "Of course. I seem to be your go-to guy today."

She gave him a quick hug. "And I appreciate all you do for me. You're my favorite brother."

"Your only brother," he tossed over his shoulder as he headed into the office suite. Then he poked his head back out. "Oh, and if we're keeping track of who's saving the day on this wedding? Me or you? I talked to Evelyn, and she is coming and bringing cookies and a cake she'd made for the cafe, and then it wasn't open today. So I've got dessert covered too. So I'd count that as four for me. None for you." He held up his fingers one by one. "Courtyard cleanup, generator picked up, generator installed, dinner, *and* dessert." He grinned as he disappeared.

"I helped with the flowers and found the mason jars," she called after him. But she really was grateful for all his help. He still kept making noise about moving out and getting a place of his own, and if he did, she'd really miss him. And not just for all the help he gave her.

CHAPTER 22

"You about ready to head out?" Jill turned to Christie, who had just finished twisting her hair back into a bun.

"I guess so. The cool shower helped, but it still is sticky, isn't it?"

"It is. But there's a slight breeze outside and Violet has chairs scattered around in the shade."

"I'm as ready as I'll ever be." Christie took one last look in the mirror. "I love that teal dress on you."

"Thanks." Jill glanced in the mirror and saw her flushed cheeks. Probably just from the heat. A cool shower hadn't done much for her, either. It wasn't because she was looking forward to spending time with Scott. Definitely not.

She and Christie headed out to the

courtyard and over to where Tony was sitting on a chair. Scott stood beside him. Violet waved to them from near the barbecue, where smoke was billowing as Rob cooked the burgers.

Christie sat down by Tony. He leaned over and kissed her. "You look great, babe."

Christie glowed from the complement. Or maybe the heat…

"I'll go grab drinks out of the cooler. What do you guys want?" Jill waited for answers.

"I'll have a beer," Tony said.

"And one for me," Christie chimed in.

"Just a soda for me. Here I'll come help you." Scott followed her over to the cooler and they grabbed the icy drinks.

She pressed her beer can to her forehead as they crossed back to the chairs. "It's going to be hot sleeping tonight."

"It is. It's much warmer tonight than last night after the storm."

Right. When she'd curled up next to him and had been all nice and cozy. "Guess we'll leave the windows open and hope for the best."

They sat down, Scott taking the chair right next to her. Rose came over. "Christie, I took a picture on my phone of your bouquet. Want to see it?"

"I do." Christie reached for the offered phone. "Oh, Rose. It's perfect. Simple. Beautiful. I love it."

Rose beamed. "I'm so glad. And I'll get the arbor all decorated tomorrow and the centerpieces all done up and on the tables."

"You've done so much. I don't know how I can ever repay your kindness." Christie jumped up and hugged Rose.

"You two just have a wonderful wedding tomorrow. That's all I ask in return."

"And you're coming, right? Please come," Christie said.

"I don't want to intrude on friends and family."

"No intrusion. And I feel like you're a friend now," Christie insisted.

"Then I'd be honored to come."

Christie's parents walked up and joined them. "This is such a lovely idea to have a barbecue since our dinner at The Cabot Hotel got canceled," Christie's mom said. "And after our attempt at a nice dinner in Sarasota last night..." Mrs. Palmer lightly touched the wrapped arm where she'd been cut. "I just didn't want to try that again."

"Wasn't that nice of Rob and Violet to do

this?" Jill glanced over at them. It looked like Rob was teasing her because Violet hip-checked him and his laugh rang out across the courtyard.

"It was. Everyone in this town is so lovely and helpful. I never would have believed when I heard what happened with the wedding coordinator, then the dress, then the storm, that you would be able to pull off this wedding so quickly. Everything is working out perfectly." Mrs. Palmer looked at her in admiration.

Jill squirmed under the praise.

Christie laughed. "Never doubt Jill when she sets her mind on something."

"Hey, I just wanted you to have the wedding you deserve."

"I think it's all going to be wonderful." Christie threw her arms wide, pointing to the arbor and the nicely cleaned-up courtyard.

Jill smiled at her friend's enthusiasm. Now, as long as there were no more surprises... She couldn't take another last-minute gotcha thrown into the wedding plans. Not a single one. She glanced around warily as if something else was going to spring up and surprise her.

Moonbeam gifted them with a brilliant sunset splashing across the sky that seemed to set the water on fire. Jill was really getting into the whole watching the sunset thing. She turned back from the view as the party was breaking up. She and Scott helped clean up the mess from the barbecue while Christie walked Tony back to his cottage. Christie's parents and Rose said good night and headed back to their cottages. When everything was cleaned up, Violet and Rob headed back to the owner's cottage.

Jill stood awkwardly in the courtyard with just Scott. She should probably head inside, too. She took one last look around the courtyard. "Looks like we've got it all ready for tomorrow."

"Would you want to take a walk on the beach? Should be nice. There's enough moonlight to see where we're walking."

Walking beside the waves sounded like a good idea. And she'd gratefully accept the breeze blowing in off the water. "That sounds nice."

They headed toward the shoreline and walked a short way down the beach. He took her hand. She liked the comfortable, warm feeling of being connected to him. The warm water lapped at her feet as they walked along, and the moon threw a path of silvery light across the waves.

The night was magical, and if she wasn't careful, she was going to fall for this man all over again.

But that was silly. They had their lives in separate—and very far apart—towns. Besides, she didn't really know him anymore, did she? Even if the last few days she'd begun to feel like she did. Like she knew him well. But this was just a week here, not enough time to really know what this was. It was friendship, that's all.

But was that all she wanted it to be? She glanced down at her hand in his.

Scott slowed down, so she slowed beside him. He stopped and looked at her so intently she caught her breath. And for a brief moment, she was sure he was going to kiss her. She held her breath, waiting.

"We need to talk," he finally said.

She wasn't sure if she was disappointed he didn't kiss her or relieved. Her thoughts and emotions bounced back and forth, waging war. She just nodded at him.

"You said we shouldn't have secrets."

She nodded yet again, afraid to speak.

"I have to tell you something."

She eyed him. He sounded so serious. "Go ahead."

"I—" He cleared his throat. "After you left and went back to college, I missed you. I missed you a lot."

"I missed you, too." And she could say that now, knowing why he'd broken up with her. What part her father had played in that.

"I… uh… I did something foolish. Just a few months after you left. After we broke up."

She looked at him pointedly.

"Um, I mean, after I broke up with you."

What did he do that was this serious? "And this foolish thing was?"

"I… I got married." His words came out in a rush and stung like a slap to her face.

"You what?" She jerked her hand out of his grasp as if his hand had scorched her.

"I got married. In Vegas. And I know that's cliche. But that's what happened."

"To someone you met in Vegas?"

"Ah… no. Someone from Sweet River Falls."

"Why didn't Christie ever tell me?" She stepped back. "Are you *still* married?"

"What? No." He shook his head. "And Christie doesn't know."

"You're not making a lot of sense."

He let out a long sigh. "And there's more."

She wasn't sure she could take more. This whole week had been one surprise after the other and she was over them. Didn't care if she ever had another surprise. Ever.

"You might as well tell me and get it over with." She paused for a moment and frowned. "So, who did you marry?"

"Ah, yes, that." He ran his fingers through his hair.

She concentrated on one lock of hair that fluttered in the breeze, sticking straight up, as she waited for his answer.

"I married… Darlene McGinnis."

"You did not." She stared at him, her mouth open. Darlene McGinnis? Had she heard him correctly?

"I… did."

"Darlene? You married Darlene? How could you? She was so hateful to me. To Christie. She's… not a nice person. Why would you *marry* her?"

He scrubbed a hand over his face. "So, she was going to Vegas for a long weekend. She invited me to come along and for some reason I'll never figure out, I said yes. I thought it might be a good distraction."

"Distraction?" She glared at him. "And the marriage part?"

"Well, we… partied. Gambled. Drank. And at some point, came up with this crazy idea to get married. We went and got our marriage license—the marriage bureau is open until midnight there—did you know that?"

Did she *care* it was open until midnight was probably a better question. None of this was making sense.

"We went and got married in one of those chapels. Not my finest hour."

She stood there in silence, taking it all in. Here she thought she'd been getting to know Scott again. But she didn't know him at all.

Not a man who could run off to Vegas and get married just months after he'd broken up with her. And to Darlene, of all people. *Darlene.* She narrowed her eyes, staring at him. "But you're divorced now?"

He let out a long sigh again. "Yes. We got back to Sweet River, and I was trying to figure out how I was going to tell my mom. Tell my friends. Determined to make the best of my foolish decision. But when we got back to my apartment, she just stood in the middle of it, turned to me, and asked me point-blank if I would leave Sweet River Falls. I said no. She said she wanted a divorce. She wasn't going to stay around Sweet River with someone who had no ambition and was never going to leave. She left town the next week and as far as I know, she's never returned." He looked out at the water, then back before continuing. "Which, considering we didn't love each other, or particularly like each other, was probably the best plan. My desire to stay in Sweet River seems to be the demise of my relationships."

"It didn't have to be with us. If you'd just told me the truth." She threw the words at him as shock and anger gurgled through her, choking her.

He nodded. "I know. Well, I know that now. Back then, I thought I was doing the only thing I could. The best thing for you."

She ignored that. "So you divorced and never told anyone?"

"I did tell Tony because I needed to talk to someone. But I swore him to secrecy. I never even told my mother. She'd be so disappointed in me."

"You keep a lot of secrets from people you say you care about. Keep secrets without giving them a chance to respond or react." She narrowed her eyes as her pulse raced through her veins.

"I... I have. But you said no more secrets, so I wanted to tell you the truth."

"But after keeping two huge secrets like these, how could I ever believe you wouldn't do it again?"

"I wouldn't."

"So you say." She struggled to hold in her anger, her hurt. *Darlene*. And it didn't matter that it happened years ago. It still stung. "We should head back. It's getting late, and it's a big day tomorrow." She spun on her heels and hurried back toward the cottages, not caring if he followed or not.

She'd prefer if he stayed out here on the beach, alone, until after the wedding. She couldn't bear to see him or talk to him right now.

She slipped into her cottage, grateful that Christie must still be over at Tony's. She went into her room and turned out the light, throwing herself across the bed. She didn't have the energy to talk to Christie right now. And besides, it was Christie's big day tomorrow. Christie didn't need to be dragged into all of this. And she sure wasn't going to tell Christie that Tony had been keeping the secret of Scott's marriage all these years, even though she grudgingly admitted it wasn't Tony's secret to tell.

How did this week get so complicated? Exhaustion spread through her and she pulled a cover over her, not even bothering to slip out of her sundress. Even that seemed to require too much effort.

She closed her eyes, but it did little to stop all the thoughts racing through her mind. And she realized she still hadn't written her speech for the reception.

CHAPTER 23

Jill crawled out of bed early the next morning and looked down at her rumpled sundress. She shrugged out of it and walked over to the light switch over on the wall, ever hopeful. She flipped it up and down and sighed. Nothing. No electricity yet.

She used her phone for a light—luckily she'd charged it up in the car yesterday—and grabbed a pair of shorts and a t-shirt from her suitcase. Quietly, she slipped outside. The sky was just beginning to lighten to a pale gray, and stars twinkled in their last grasp of the night. The tiniest breeze breeze cooled her skin as she headed for the beach.

She found Rose in her usual spot and

dropped down beside her, comforted by their morning ritual.

"Morning." Rose smiled at her. "Glad you joined me again."

"I'm going to miss these early mornings and watching the day awaken. I never take time for this back home."

"Maybe you should."

"Maybe." But not likely. She was always rushing off to work, coffee in hand, hurrying to be one of the first people to the office. Always competing for the I-was-here-first designation or honor or whatever. Hoping that upper management would see what a hard worker she was.

The same reason she went to work on the weekends. Really, almost every single day with no break. She frowned. Why had she thought all of that was so very important? So important it ruled her whole life?

"So, today's the big day." Rose interrupted her thoughts.

"It is. I'd hoped the electricity would be back on."

"Ah, it will be what it is. On or off. I'm sure they'll still have a beautiful wedding."

"I hope so." Why was she sitting here? She should be writing the stupid speech for the reception. But still, she just sat and stared at the sky.

"So I saw you talking to Scott last night. You seem to be getting along well."

She let out a long sigh. "We were. I took your advice and asked him about the breakup. It's a long story, but my father was involved and I think Scott thought he was doing the right thing. But I still wish he would have just talked to me. Not kept it a secret."

Rose just sat and let her talk.

"And then… I found out last night when we were taking a walk on the beach that he… he got married right after he broke up with me."

"Oh?"

"Yes, but it wasn't someone he'd been dating before. It was—get this—one of those last-minute weddings in one of those Vegas chapels." She picked up a shell and threw it across the sand. "And he married this woman that… let's just say, is not a nice person. She was so mean to me and to Christie when we were younger. And she always picked on other girls for being a bit overweight or wearing glasses or whatever she decided to pick on. Just… not nice. How could he marry her?"

"I don't know. We sometimes make foolish choices when we're young."

"Well, that was one big foolish choice. And as soon as they got back home, she asked him for a divorce. He never told anyone except Tony. He never even told his mother and they are really close. I don't know why he keeps secrets from people he professes to care so much about. I just… I just don't trust him. I don't think I ever could."

Rose looked at her intently. "Sometimes we make mistakes in our youth. Decisions we regret later. Decisions we can't believe we made when we look back on them from the wisdom of our age. It would be nice if people we care about could forgive us. Especially as the years go by."

"But how would I ever trust him not to keep another secret?"

"I don't know. You just have to find a way to trust. To believe in him. The man he is now. Realize that people change and grow and learn from their mistakes. But only you can decide if you want to trust him. To take a chance with him. Is that what you want? Do you want to see if you can have a relationship with him again?"

"Wow, you ask the hard questions, don't you?" She gave Rose a weak smile.

"I feel like it's always better to face problems head-on. Well, I do now. I wish my younger self would have treated difficult situations better. Talked it out instead of getting angry. It's always better to work things out with people you care about."

"I just don't know. I don't know anything. How I feel about him. If I even want a simple friendship with him."

"You don't have to figure it all out at once. But you do have a chance to talk to him more since you're both here."

"But today is the wedding. I need to concentrate on that." She stood up and brushed the sand off her shorts. "I think I'll head back and see if Violet made coffee. I really need coffee to face today."

Rose stood. "I'll go with you. I'm pretty much a morning equals coffee person myself."

Jill crossed the courtyard back toward her cottage after getting her coveted cup of coffee. She slipped inside and went to find Christie and give her the large mug she'd brought for her.

"Oh, thanks. I need this." Christie took the mug. "I've been here reading through your lists." She grinned. "I do think almost everything is ready. Rose will work on the rest of the flowers today."

"And you have to get ready."

"I will in a while. I'm just going to enjoy the morning. I told Tony he can't see me today until the wedding. I'm just old-fashioned enough to want that."

"I'll run interference for you."

Jill went over and rinsed some dishes and mindlessly cleaned up the kitchen area, even though it didn't really need it.

"You're kind of quiet today. What's wrong?" Christie asked as she picked up her wedding shoes off the floor by her chair and stared at them.

"Nothing."

Christie held up the shoes. "Do you think I should wear these? What was I thinking picking out heels like these to walk on the uneven ground out there? I think either Tony or I should be walking steadily, and it sure isn't going to be him on those crutches."

"The shoes are pretty, though."

"They are… but you know what? I'm going to go barefoot."

"You are?" She looked at her friend in surprise. Everyone was surprising her this week.

"Sure, why not? It's a beach wedding, after all. And I love going barefoot. Don't get much chance in Colorado."

"Okay, then. Barefoot it is."

"So you will, too, right?"

"Um… if that's what you want."

"It is." Christie twirled around, facing her. "Now tell me what's wrong."

"Nothing," she repeated, trying to sound more sure of herself.

"You're not telling me the truth. Not the whole story."

"It's nothing."

"Yes. It is. It's something. Tony told me about how your father jumped in and kind of wrecked things between you and Scott. But I can't really blame Scott. Can you? He was so young."

"He should have talked to me."

"Probably. But he did what he thought was the right thing. There isn't anything wrong with doing what you really think is the right thing.

Even if later it turns out it wasn't a great decision."

She looked over at her friend. "And how did you get so smart?"

"One of us has to be the smart one. I was tired of people thinking it was always you with your fancy job and fancy condo."

She looked carefully at Christie. "Do you really feel like that? That people think I'm smarter or something than you? Because... well, I'm not. And you have all the practical good sense. And creativity. And everyone—and I mean *everyone*—loves you. I think I'm too..." She shrugged. "Brusque. Exacting. Though I never expect more from anyone than I do myself."

"But sometimes people don't want to do things your way. That doesn't mean their way is wrong."

She frowned. She knew she was a bit judgmental. Okay, maybe even critical. Maybe even of things she had no right to judge. "I'm kind of a piece of work, aren't I?"

"You know I love you. Just like you are." Christie got up and hugged her. "And I don't believe there is even one other person in the world who could have pulled off a wedding for me. Not like this. Not with all the problems we've had. And you overcame every single one of them. That's your strength. You don't give up. Not on things you're trying to make happen." Christie paused and stepped back. "And maybe you shouldn't give up on Scott. Not without at least seeing where it might lead this time. At least think about it."

"Well, there's another detail about his past. You won't believe this. He married Darlene McGinnis."

Christie's eyes widened. "Darlene?" She sank slowly back down on her chair. "Darlene McGinnis? I had no idea."

It somehow comforted her that Christie was as shocked as she'd been. "Yeah, in one of those Vegas wedding chapels. After a bit too much of a good time partying."

"Wow, never knew that."

"They divorced almost before the ink was dry on the marriage certificate." Not that it made it any better. Darlene McGinnis! Of all the women in the world.

"I didn't know about it, but I'm glad he told you." Christie frowned, pursing her lips. "Hm, I wonder if that's why he always only has one drink now. I've never seen him have more than one. Did you notice that?"

She thought back on the times they'd been together and his hesitancy when she'd offered him a drink. "No, I didn't notice at the time, but I think you're right."

"Guess he learned his lesson with drinking and making foolish decisions. Anyway, I'm glad he told you. I know you said you don't want any more secrets."

"But if he could keep a secret like that from everyone—he's never even told his mother—how can I ever trust him not to keep secrets from me?"

"Or you could look at it that he trusts you enough to tell his deepest secret to." Christie pinned her with a hard stare. "You could think of it that way."

She frowned. "But—"

"Jill, I love you. I do. But people make mistakes. People change. You need to accept that. You always want everything planned out, and sometimes life just doesn't work out that way. Scott's a great guy. And I'm pretty sure he still cares about you. A lot. I think you should talk to him. See if you can sort things out."

Christie rose. "I should go start to get ready. But think about what I said."

She let out a long sigh. Tough love from both Rose and Christie today. "Okay, I will. But not now. Now is all about you. Let's get you ready for this wedding we're having."

CHAPTER 24

Jill walked outside later that afternoon while Christie was taking a cool shower. She lifted her hair off the nape of her neck. If the breeze didn't pick up soon, it was going to be a very hot, sticky wedding.

Scott walked out on the porch of his cottage and saw her. He ducked back inside without saying a word. Probably just as well. Then a minute later he appeared and strode across the distance, stepping up onto her porch.

"I know you're mad at me. Disappointed. I'm always disappointing people. But... I went into town yesterday and got this for you. I didn't want your birthday to go by without any celebration. I thought it might give you some

243

inspiration for writing the speech for the reception." He held out a small box.

She took the box and opened the lid. "Oh, a fountain pen. It's lovely."

He grinned. "With purple ink."

"This is so nice. Thank you." And even though it was hard to admit, it thrilled her that he'd remembered her birthday. And found the perfect gift. She lifted her face and stared at him for a long minute. "You know what? I'm not going to write it again. I'm going to wing it."

His eyes widened. "What did you say? Jill of the master plan for everything is going to wing it?"

"Yes. I am. She's my best friend. I could talk about her forever. I've got this."

He looked at her admiringly. "Good for you, Jillybean. I'm proud of you."

Suddenly, they heard shouting and clapping. Violet rushed out of the office and called across the courtyard. "It's on. The electricity is back! Close your windows. Get those air conditioners running."

"Yes." She did a quick fist pump and turned to Scott. "I should let Christie know if she doesn't yet. But she's been hopping up to flick the light switch like every other minute. I was going to suggest to her that if she left a light on, she'd know immediately when the electricity was back. But I think the jumping up and checking is good for all her nervous energy." She turned to head inside but turned back to Scott. "But one other thing."

"What's that?"

"Just because I'm not writing a speech…" She grinned at him. "I'll still take the fountain pen. Thank you."

"Happy birthday, Jillybean."

She gripped the pen in her hand as she walked back into the cottage.

Jill stood at the end of the aisle with Christie. "You ready for this?"

"I am. I feel like I've been waiting half my life for this. Too bad Tony and I didn't figure this out years ago." She smiled.

"I'm so happy for you. For both of you."

"I'm glad you made it this week. I wasn't sure you would. You've been so busy."

"I know, and I'm sorry. I promise to make more time to come back to Sweet River."

"I'm going to hold you to that promise."

"Okay, there's my cue. I'm headed down the aisle." She turned to Christie's dad. "She's all yours, Mr. Palmer."

She headed down the aisle to the arbor, where Scott was standing by Tony's side. Tony's eyes clouded with tears as Christie and her father walked down the aisle. Jill choked back tears of her own. The sky flooded with colors of blue and orange above them. The breeze picked up just enough to cool, not enough to mess with Christie's perfectly styled hair.

Yes, the wedding had worked out perfectly. She'd given her best friend the wedding she deserved.

She looked over and saw Scott smiling at her. Her mouth crept up in a small smile. He looked ridiculously handsome in gray slacks and a white shirt. She glanced down, and her small smile broke into a full grin. Both he and Tony were barefoot, too.

Then the wedding was over and Christie and Tony walked back down the aisle, Tony thankfully making it without a stumble.

Scott crossed over and took her arm. "Beautiful wedding you pulled off," he whispered in her ear.

She blushed, happy with the compliment.

Happy to be walking beside him, her arm tucked through his. When they got to the end of the aisle, she turned to him. "We should talk. But not tonight. Tonight is for Christie and Tony."

He nodded. "I'd like to talk, too. Very much."

"Tomorrow morning on the beach? Sunrise?"

"It's a date." He nodded, then rushed over to Tony to get him a chair and rescue the crutch he was waving around as he talked.

CHAPTER 25

Rose watched the lovely ceremony, pleased with how the flowers accented the arbor and the simple beauty of the mason jar arrangements on the tables. She'd been happy to help. To contribute to such an important day. To feel part of it.

So many memories danced through her head and her heart. It had been a perfect evening, just like this one when she and Emmett had stood in almost that exact spot and gotten married. The sunset had been glorious, with shades of deep yellow and orange bursting through the fluffy clouds. They hadn't had a crowd like this, though. Just her and Emmett, along with her sister, Emmett's best friend, and the minister from a small chapel in town.

It had been the most wonderful evening of her life. Her whole life had stretched out before her and she'd looked forward to years of happiness. And they'd had many years of happiness, though they'd had their share of pain. Like when they found out she couldn't have children. Emmett had been so supportive, though she knew he wanted children. He'd never blamed her, but she'd seen the pain in his eyes.

But they'd worked through it. Lived with it. Had a good life together.

She didn't have many regrets with her life.

Well, one.

Her sister. The one she hadn't seen in more than forty years.

CHAPTER 26

Jill awoke suddenly the next morning trying to figure out why she was so excited. The wedding was over. It had all gone off without a hitch. Even her speech, which she'd just winged it like Scott had suggested, turned out well. Though she admitted Scott's was better. Plenty of laughs with his. Hers had been more sentimental. But she'd done it. Risked winging it without a big old long list with everything planned out.

Then she remembered. Knew why she was excited.

She was meeting Scott on the beach. Jumping out of bed, she wrestled a brush through her hair, brushed her teeth, and put on shorts and a top. She hurried out to the beach.

There was Rose, sitting in her normal spot. But no Scott.

She went over to Rose. "I'm supposed to meet Scott out here this morning. Have you seen him?"

"No."

"I listened to you, and I listened to Christie. I need more honest, straight-shooters in my life. I want you to know how much I appreciate being able to talk to you this week. You're a good listener."

"I'm glad I could help." Rose nodded toward a lone figure walking toward them from way down the beach. "I bet that's your young man right now. He must have gotten up early and taken a walk while he waited for you."

She didn't really think of Scott as a young man, but she guessed it was all in a person's perspective. "I think I'll go walk down and meet him."

"I think you should. Go on." Rose shooed her away.

Jill hurried down the beach toward Scott, watching the grin spread across his face as he saw her.

"Hey, you," he said softly as she reached him.

"Hey, you," she replied, feeling her own grin stretch ear to ear.

"Wanna sit?"

She nodded, and they sat on the beach as the sky lightened in front of them and a lone gull swept past in an arc high above.

"So, you wanted to talk." He leaned back on his elbows.

"I did. I do. I mean…" Suddenly the words wouldn't come. She didn't know what to say. How to even start.

"Wing it." He grinned at her.

She took a deep breath. "I'm sorry for so much. For years of being mad at you for breaking up with me. For how I reacted when you told me about Darlene. It must have been hard to tell me that."

"It was. I knew I was risking messing up the fragile bond you and I had going."

"And I was angry. Not just because it was Darlene—and really? Darlene?"

"I know, I know." He held up his hands. "What was I thinking? Well, I wasn't thinking. That's what the problem was."

"But it hurt that you could go and get married right after our breakup."

"I'm so—"

She held up her hand and stopped him. "No, don't apologize again. I'm glad you told me. I said no more secrets, and you did what I asked."

"I won't ever keep a secret from you again." He reached out and took her hand. "So, do you think we could start over? Try again? See where this is headed?"

"There's just not enough time." She let out a long sigh. "I'm scheduled to fly out in the morning. Our timing is impossible. I think our destinies are just forever crossed."

"I think people make their own destinies. By the choices they make. With what they learn from their past mistakes."

"But you're all the way across the country in Sweet River. We just don't have time…"

"Make time. Stay here for another week. Get to know me again. Give us a chance."

"I can't just stay another week. I have to get back. I have plans already made for work next week."

"Change them." He challenged her with his stare. "Give us a chance, Jillybean. Be spontaneous."

"I…" She stopped herself. She was getting ready to say she couldn't. But she could. It was really up to her. She had months of vacation banked because she never took it. She had coworkers who could cover the work. Though, how might taking another week off affect her possible promotion?

But then... she suddenly didn't care. She wasn't sure the promotion was the right thing for her, anyway. How many more hours a week could the job take of her life? She had no life outside of work. And was that any way to live?

He sat patiently, waiting.

"Okay, I'll do it. I'll take another week. Do you think Violet can get us cottages for the week?"

"Um, I might have already checked. But she only has one. Will that be a problem?"

She chewed her bottom lip. "No... but that doesn't mean that..."

He laughed. "It's a two-bedroom. You can have your own room."

"Okay, then. I'll stay."

"Yes." He jumped up, reached a hand down, and pulled her up beside him. "And one more thing."

"Yes?" Her breath caught in her throat and her heart pounded.

"In an effort to see where all this is heading, do you think it would be okay if I kissed you?"

She grinned. "I thought you'd never ask."

He kissed her. And kissed her again.

Then he pulled back ever so slightly. "And I do have one more secret I have to share."

She eyed him warily. "I don't think I can take another surprise."

"I'm hoping you'll like this one."

"And it is…?"

"I love you. I always have. Never stopped."

"Oh, Scotty." Tears sprang up in her eyes. Her heart soared as happiness flooded through her. He touched her face with a caress as soft as the breeze, then held her close as the sunrise crept across the sky and the waves rolled to the shore. And everything was perfectly right in her world, ensconced in his arms. And for the first time in more than thirty years, she knew she was right where she belonged.

What's up next in the Blue Heron Series? The Bookshop near the Coast is next. Collette, the owner of the bookshop, is at a crossroads. Can a stranger who comes to stay at the cottages help her sort it out? And what about Rose? We learn some more of Rose's secrets. And is Rob ever going to move out of Violet's owner suite and into a place of his own? Are he and Evelyn going to get serious? Get Bookshop near the Coast and find out.

Also, after I finished this book and sent it off to my editor, I decided I really wanted to wrap up Scott and Jill's story back in Sweet River Falls. I offered up a bonus epilogue to my newsletter subscribers. If you're not on my list and want to get on my newsletter and read any bonus content, sign up here: kaycorrell.com/bonus2

And if you haven't read the Sweet River series, start with book one, A Dream to Believe In.

As always, I appreciate all of you. Hope you're enjoying my stories.

Until next time, Kay

ALSO BY KAY CORRELL

COMFORT CROSSING ~ THE SERIES

The Shop on Main - Book One

The Memory Box - Book Two

The Christmas Cottage - A Holiday Novella (Book 2.5)

The Letter - Book Three

The Christmas Scarf - A Holiday Novella (Book 3.5)

The Magnolia Cafe - Book Four

The Unexpected Wedding - Book Five

The Wedding in the Grove (crossover short story between series - Josephine and Paul from The Letter.)

LIGHTHOUSE POINT ~ THE SERIES

Wish Upon a Shell - Book One

Wedding on the Beach - Book Two

Love at the Lighthouse - Book Three

Cottage near the Point - Book Four

Return to the Island - Book Five

Bungalow by the Bay - Book Six

Christmas Comes to Lighthouse Point - Book Seven

CHARMING INN ~ Return to Lighthouse Point

One Simple Wish - Book One

Two of a Kind - Book Two

Three Little Things - Book Three

Four Short Weeks - Book Four

Five Years or So - Book Five

Six Hours Away - Book Six

Charming Christmas - Book Seven

SWEET RIVER ~ THE SERIES

A Dream to Believe in - Book One

A Memory to Cherish - Book Two

A Song to Remember - Book Three

A Time to Forgive - Book Four

A Summer of Secrets - Book Five

A Moment in the Moonlight - Book Six

MOONBEAM BAY ~ THE SERIES

The Parker Women - Book One

The Parker Cafe - Book Two

A Heather Parker Original - Book Three

The Parker Family Secret - Book Four

Grace Parker's Peach Pie - Book Five

The Perks of Being a Parker - Book Six

BLUE HERON COTTAGES ~ THE SERIES

Memories of the Beach - Book One

Walks along the Shore - Book Two

Bookshop near the Coast - Book Three

Plus more to come!

WIND CHIME BEACH ~ A stand-alone novel

INDIGO BAY ~ Save by getting Kay's complete collection of stories previously published separately in the multi-author Indigo Bay series. The three stories are all interconnected.

Sweet Days by the Bay - the collection

ABOUT THE AUTHOR

Kay writes sweet, heartwarming stories that are a cross between women's fiction and contemporary romance. She is known for her charming small towns, quirky townsfolk, and enduring strong friendships between the women in her books.

Kay lives in the Midwest of the U.S. and can often be found out and about with her camera, taking a myriad of photographs which she likes to incorporate into her book covers. When not lost in her writing or photography, she can be found spending time with her ever-supportive husband, knitting, or playing with her puppies —two cavaliers and one naughty but adorable Australian shepherd. Kay and her husband also love to travel. When it comes to vacation time, she is torn between a nice trip to the beach or the mountains—but the mountains only get considered in the summer—she swears she's allergic to snow.

Learn more about Kay and her books at
kaycorrell.com

While you're there, sign up for her newsletter to
hear about new releases, sales, and giveaways.

WHERE TO FIND ME:
kaycorrell.com
authorcontact@kaycorrell.com

Join my Facebook Reader Group. We have lots
of fun and you'll hear about sales and new
releases first!
www.facebook.com/groups/KayCorrell/

I love to hear from my readers. Feel free to
contact me at authorcontact@kaycorrell.com

facebook.com/KayCorrellAuthor

instagram.com/kaycorrell

pinterest.com/kaycorrellauthor

amazon.com/author/kaycorrell

bookbub.com/authors/kay-correll

Made in the USA
Monee, IL
12 September 2022

13853852R00159